CL

Revised Dreams

ARMADA

CLASS OF '88

4

Revised Dreams

Linda A. Cooney

ARMADA

First published in USA by Scholastic Inc. in 1987
First published in UK by Armada in 1988

Armada is an imprint of
the Children's Division, part of
the Collins Publishing Group,
8 Grafton Street, London W1X 3LA

Printed and bound in Great Britain by
William Collins Sons & Co. Ltd, Glasgow

Revised Dreams

CHAPTER 1

"You're Nick Rhodes, aren't you? My friend Jennifer really wants to meet you."

"Sara, shhh. I do not."

Whispers, giggles, and muffled shrieks. Nick slowly turned around. Two freshman girls, one in a pink sundress, the other with braces and a dopey rock band sweat shirt, were only a few feet away. When he looked at them, they both turned scarlet and rammed into the lockers behind them. The one in the sundress hopped from one foot to the other and poked her friend. "He's looking at you. Say something!"

"Sara, stop it. You say something!"

"Jennifer!"

Nick managed a smile, one that made them both become even more frantic. Not taking their eyes off him, they backed down the hall, stumbling into the horde of seniors and parents who were heading toward the cafeteria. Finally the two girls turned and ran.

"Freshmen," Nick sighed. Had he been like that once? Self-conscious, not knowing how to act, being silly and embarrassed both at the same time. He wouldn't trade places with them for anything. Redwood High was such familiar territory to him now. His turf. Whether he was on the football field or in the newspaper office, the classroom or the B-ball court, he was right at home. Of course, it wouldn't be home much longer. Six more weeks, and it was bye-bye Redwood High. No more bells ringing, people telling him not to hang out in the hall. . . .

"Hey, Nick!"

. . . no more having your own locker. . . .

"HEY, RHODES! ARE YOU ASLEEP OR SOMETHING?"

Nick jumped and then turned around, looking toward the cafeteria. Greg Kendall was blocking the cafeteria door, a big grin on his face. "Boy, are you getting spacy. Are you coming to this tea thing?"

"I'll be there," Nick yelled. "I'm just waiting for my folks."

"Okay, but you better hurry," Greg called back. "We might drink up all that yummy tea the service club made."

Nick laughed and leaned back. The hall was really filling up now. It was the day of the senior/parent tea, when all the seniors and their folks met for an after-school offering of watery tea and cafeteria coffee cake and were informed about the events between now and graduation.

2

This was considered the kickoff, the starting gun, the beginning of the end of it all for the class of '88.

"Hey, Nick," Jeff Greenberg shouted. He was walking down the hall at lightning speed. That was the way Jeff was — fast. Fast at everything, including the articles he wrote with Nick for the newspaper. "What are you waiting for?" Jeff called as he sped by. "Your parents are probably already in the caf."

"Just avoiding the crowd," Nick smiled. Jeff shrugged but barely slowed down.

Nick knew his parents hadn't beat him inside. He'd been waiting in the hall since before the final bell. He could hear Miss Meyer inside telling everyone to take their seats. There were fewer people in the hall now. Just latecomers scrambling, a few lost parents, and the teachers who stood at the door herding people in. Finally the bell rang, and the cafeteria doors were being pulled closed. Nick took one last look up and down the hall — his parents still hadn't shown. Nick had to make his move now. He slunk past the doors into the cafeteria.

"Welcome, everyone! Will you please get settled so we can start," Miss Meyer spoke into the microphone. She was at the podium right next to where Nick walked in. "We have a lot to do." Her voice echoed and was answered by screams of feedback. The seniors moaned, and their parents covered their ears.

Nick sauntered toward the back, and about ten hands waved for his attention. The jocks were saving him a seat, as was Sally Ann Stormis, a

3

pretty girl in his government class, and some of Jeff and Nick's other newspaper pals. But as much as Nick liked all those kids, he found himself heading to the very back, toward Celia, his cousin. This year he spent all his time with acquaintances, casual buddies from the paper or B ball or class. Celia certainly wasn't as easy to be with, or as much fun as Jeff or Sally or Greg, but with his parents not showing up, something inside made Nick want to be next to someone he'd known for a very long time.

Celia was sitting by herself, sorting through a stack of three-by-five cards. Her perfect face was squinched up in concentration.

"Hi," he said, plopping down next to her. "What are you doing?"

Celia glanced up. She had the same striking blonde looks as Nick, except that her eyes were soft turquoise where Nick's were brilliant green. "Meg roped me into helping with this prom fashion show right after the tea," she said. "I'm trying to get the model order figured out so it all goes smoothly, and I can get out of here. I'm meeting Derek over at the café."

Nick nodded. Celia had been waitressing part-time at Redwood College and attracting the attention of more than a few college boys. With each flirtation she grew less and less interested in high school. Derek Jamison, some frat guy, was her latest. Since meeting him a couple of weeks ago, she didn't seem to have much time for senior activities. Nick found her whole attitude a little weird, considering that only a year ago she'd been

4

one of the most social and popular girls in the entire class.

"Where's Meg?" Nick asked. That same odd feeling that made him want to sit in the back with Celia made him need to check on the rest of the old gang.

Celia had her face back in her cards. "Up front with Patrick."

Nick started to bob up, then forced himself to stay seated. His eyes had locked on Meg's instantly, as if she were bugged with a homing device. Meg McCall. Her dark hair was pulled back in a glossy braid, and she had on her track team sweat shirt. Her parents were with her, and Meg was leaning over a huge stack of books, writing something on an official-looking clipboard. Patrick, Meg's boyfriend, was there, too, with his parents.

"Meg," Nick whispered only to himself.

The tea began with announcements about grad night and the senior talent show. Since Patrick was class vice-president, he got up to talk about ordering diplomas and caps and gowns. But Nick kept his eyes on Meg. She didn't watch Patrick while he gave his announcements but instead, made notes and checked lists. She stopped working only to wave at their old friend Allie. Then Meg made a goofy face at Sean, another of their childhood gang, and at his girl friend Brooke. Me, too, Nick had the sudden urge to call. Complete the circle and look at me, too. But, of course, she didn't wave to him or make a face or even look in his direction.

Nick gave up and read the senior calendar that had been left at his place. He tried to listen to the announcements, but he was suddenly too restless to really pay attention. Then something hit him. He looked around the cafeteria. "How weird." He nudged his cousin. "Cici, you want to know something weird?"

Instead of answering, Celia pitched forward and shushed him. She was listening intently as Patrick announced that prom tickets would only be on sale for one more week. "Only one more week," Celia repeated. "I'd better work on Derek. So far he hasn't seemed very excited about going."

"Do you care? I thought you were sick of high school."

"I am. But this is an exception. It's the prom, Nick. Our one and only senior prom."

"Sorry."

When Miss Meyer stepped up to the mike again and rambled about finals and transcripts, Celia went back to her fashion show cards. "What were you going to say, Nick?"

"Hm?"

"About something being weird."

"Oh, yeah." Nick took another look around. The cafeteria had been decorated for this meeting with flowers and white paper tablecloths, but he could still see the scuffs and splats and stains that had been added to this place since they were freshmen and the school was brand-new. "I just realized that this is the first time we've all been together — in the same place, I mean — since junior year."

Celia wrinkled her nose. "No, it isn't. We had that senior assembly before spring break. How could you forget that? It was the most boring two hours of my life."

"Not the senior class. Us."

"Us?"

"The five of us."

Celia put down her index cards. "Oh."

"You, me, and Meg at that assembly. But Allie was at play rehearsal, and I think Sean went to that special electronics workshop in San Francisco."

"You mean. . . ." Her voice caught. "Us."

"Yeah. Us. The five of us."

"Nick, you remember that?" She rolled her eyes. "You remember which of us was at some assembly and which of us wasn't?"

"Don't you?"

A flicker of doubt passed over her face. "No," she decided. "It's really not a big deal with me anymore."

Nick knew it shouldn't have been a big deal with him, either. Sure, they'd grown up together in Redwood Hills, the five of them — he, Celia, Meg, Allie, and Sean — and they stayed close until the spring of junior year, when Allie had run away, when he and Meg . . . when he and Meg had almost figured it out, almost gotten together. Nick let out a painful sigh. That was over now. Just like the five of them were over.

"I guess Allie's doing okay," Celia said coolly about her ex-best friend. "I can't believe Sean and Brooke are still together, though. I never thought that would last." She craned her neck to see where

Sean and Brooke were sitting. They were both surrounded by their parents. Sean's red head leaned into Brooke's blonde curls. Allie was next to them, and the three of them were whispering together and stifling laughter. "I still think she's kind of a dork."

"I don't," Nick answered quickly.

Nick was tempted to add that maybe if Celia had the guts to admit that she'd been wrong about Brooke — that Brooke wasn't a dork but a bright, terrific girl who was proud of being different — maybe then the five of them might have had a chance. But then again, there was a lot more to it than just Sean and Brooke, and maybe Celia was right. Maybe the whole thing really was no big deal. The Beatles had broken up, hadn't they? That's what Sean said when he and Nick discussed it. You can't expect people to stay together forever.

They listened for a while. Joanne Fantozzi, class president, announced the senior awards assembly and Miss Meyer got back up to talk about the final selection for valedictorian and the graduation ceremony.

"Where are your folks?" Celia asked, too distracted now to listen or concentrate on the fashion show.

"I guess something came up." Nick shrugged, looking away. "You know how busy they get. How about your mom?"

"Are you serious?"

"Why not?"

"Needless to say, I told her not to come."

Nick didn't react. It had been like this for

years. Celia was embarrassed because her single mom talked too loudly, dressed like a wild teen-ager, and worked as a hairdresser downtown. Nick always thought it was kind of cool to have a mother who looked like one of your classmates — especially compared to his mom, who wore pressed skirts and nylon stockings to work in the garden. When his dad was a state senator Nick had assumed that his mom was always keeping up some kind of image. But his dad had lost his last election and was practicing law in town again, and she seemed to be the same. Well, at least on the outside she was the same.

"Anyway," Celia continued, "Mom knows now to stay away. She doesn't even ask anymore. Thank God." She checked her watch. "I hope this gets over soon. I have to be at work at five. And I can't afford to miss Derek."

Nick shoved his senior calendar away. Think-ing about his parents made Nick wish that this meeting would be over. He knew this graduation business was just starting, but he'd already had his fill. What was so great about getting out into the world anyway? Whoever said it was going to be any better than it was right here?

Finally the service club members appeared carrying trays of coffee cake and pushing carts of tea. The important business was finished. Parents were standing up to shake hands, and Sam Pond was going from table to table trying to get kids to help him paint CLASS OF '88 on the street in front of the school. Before Sam could reach him, Nick pushed back his chair and said to Celia, "I'm outta here."

"You're not staying for the fashion show?"

He smiled and patted her shoulder. Believe it or not, I'm not too worried about what I'm going to wear to the prom." She looked puzzled, so he added, "I have to start thinking about this article for *The Guardian*. They want me to do a farewell piece, what it means to be a senior and all that."

"Okay. See you tomorrow."

"Yeah."

She went back to her index cards while Nick quietly slipped out the side door. As soon as he hit the warm spring air he started to jog, raising his arms, stretching his long legs, and letting his head fall back. He jogged all the way to the parking lot.

When he made it to his car, he drove straight home, singing loudly with the radio until he pulled into his driveway. He snapped off the music and sat for a moment while the engine pinged, and Hughie, his dog, raced out to meet him. His parents' cars were in the driveway. Both of them. Nick had a sudden urge to turn the radio back up, to turn the engine back on and drive up Capitola Mountain, or to walk into the house singing at the top of his lungs.

Instead he got out, patted Hughie, and marched normally up to the kitchen door. But even before he stuck the key in, he heard it. Voices. Hard, angry voices. Words that in a million years Nick didn't want to hear again.

And in that moment, Nick knew that if this is what it meant to grow up, to graduate and become an adult, then he'd rather spend the rest of his life in his old childhood tree house with his toy soldiers and Hughie. He also knew that his parents didn't have an excuse for not showing up at the tea. And he wouldn't ask for one. It was all too obvious. They were fighting again.

CHAPTER 2

"Brooke, you should wear something like this to the prom."

"But Allie, that's a nightgown."

"I know. Be daring. Wait! I could be your fashion consultant."

"You, Al? I mean you're a great friend and a terrific actress but. . . ."

"Come on, I'd be great. Hey, Sean, I could pick out your clothes, too."

"No, thanks, Al. You'd probably put me in pajamas with feet or those slippers that look like rabbits."

"Oh, yes, perfect!"

Allie peered back into her copy of *Vogue*, which she had stacked on top of the latest *Rolling Stone*, which was draped over the May issue of *Interview*. She, Sean, and Brooke were huddled together in McGraw's Newstand, a narrow old store in the downtown mall that smelled like cigars and had almost every magazine known to man. They often started their Saturdays in Mc-Graw's, checking out the latest in everything from world news to far-out fashion to *New Yorker* cartoons.

"Really, Sean," Allie insisted, "since I'm not going to the prom, I should at least leave my mark by picking out outfits for you two."

Sean closed the *HiFi News* he'd been reading and ruffled Brooke's blonde curls. "What do you think, Brooke? Are we brave enough?"

Brooke snuggled back against him. They both stared at Allie, taking in her streaked hair, the single long earring, baggy sundress, man's tie, Mexican sandals and lace-trimmed socks. Allie took a step back to show herself off, posing with her hands behind her head.

"I guess I couldn't do too much worse on my own," Brooke teased.

Sean and Allie came back at the same time, "You wanna bet?"

Brooke looked down at her own pink overalls. They all laughed.

"As long as Brooke doesn't dress like that," Sean teased, pointing to a photo in the magazine Brooke was holding. It was a man in full fishing gear holding a huge spotted trout.

"Brooke, what are you looking at now?"

Brooke closed the cover and showed it to Allie. In the twenty minutes they'd been in McGraw's, Brooke had browsed through *Theater Crafts*, *Popular Mechanics*, *Road and Track*, and three issues of *Wonder Woman* comics. Now she was looking at *Fly Fishing for Trout*.

Allie shook her head and said to Sean, "Your girl friend is very weird."

"I know," Sean said proudly.

Grinning, Brooke placed the fishing magazine back on the rack. "That's me." She headed for the door. "And we'd better start shopping, or this weird girl is going to have to wear her weird overalls to her senior prom." She turned back. "Which, come to think of it, may not be such a bad idea."

Allie laughed again — a loud, goofy Allie laugh that made old Mr. McGraw look up from his crossword puzzle and laugh, too.

The girls waited for Sean to pay for his *HiFi News*, then marched out together, blinking, into the bright noon sun. They looked up and down the walkway, deciding which way to head first. The downtown mall was where all the old specialty shops were, like McGraw's or Sean's parents' bicycle store or Second Hand Rose, the used clothing store that was Allie's favorite. The walkway was lined with palm trees and flowers. It always smelled like fresh bread. They all preferred the old mall to the sterile indoor shopping center that housed the big department stores and fourplex movie theaters.

"Hold on a sec," Sean insisted, pointing to a cart that sold homemade cinnamon rolls. "I need a fuel injection — especially if I have to listen to Allie's fashion ideas." He hopped over a wooden bench and leaped across a flower bed, returning quickly with four hot rolls stacked in one hand.

"For us?"

Sean had already taken a huge bite out of the

top one. He was so tall and energetic that it took constant food intake to maintain the muscle he'd put on through years of hard cycling and hiking the hills. "One for you. Two for me." He winked at Allie. "Just like when we were kids."

Brooke and Allie looked at one another and shrugged.

"You know how I'd love to look at clothes with you two," Sean said sarcastically. He hiked himself up to sit on a concrete retaining wall, then helped Brooke hop up next to him. Allie sat on the back of the bench beneath them, and they tore into their rolls. "But I have to go over to Payson's Stereo, to see about renting a tape machine for the senior talent show. I'm doing the sound effects."

"Have to? Like it's such torture for you to spend time in a stereo store," Brooke teased. Sean loved anything electronic, especially audio equipment. He'd built practically his entire stereo system from scratch. "Now, finding a dress for the prom. For me, that's torture."

"Hey, I only got involved in this whole talent show thing for Allie — so she'll have a chance to show off her brilliant acting talents one last time." Sean kissed Brooke's cheek, depositing a dot of white frosting. "And so you can build one last inspiring stage set."

Brooke handed him half her roll and licked her fingers. "Did you guys know that Celia finally volunteered to help with costumes for the talent show?"

Allie's face, which lately looked animated and bright, went slack. After the trouble she'd had

15

junior year, she'd needed to break away from Celia, even though they'd been so close since they were little. There were times, though, when Allie missed her old friend so much it ached. But Celia hadn't seemed interested in patching things up with Brooke or Sean or Allie herself. "Really? You mean Celia'd really want to get involved in something for the boring old class of eighty-eight?"

"Her name was on the list."

"Meg talked her into it," Sean said. "Maybe Celia's getting back into things. Meg says all Celia talks about is how she wants to go to the prom with some frat guy she's dating."

"Frat guy," Allie giggled. "Ooh. Big muscles."

"Not from what Meg says," Sean answered. He lived across the street from Meg and Celia. But this year he hardly ever talked to Celia, either. "Al, are you going to finish your roll?"

Allie handed the last third of her cinnamon bun up to him. "How come you never get fat?"

"Strength of character." Sean ate it in two bites. "Anyway, Meg said Celia is dying to go to the prom with this guy."

"Well, the prom," Brooke broke in, "that's more understandable. No matter how sick of high school you are, most everybody still wants to go to the prom." Instantly she lowered her pretty face and touched Allie's shoulder. "Not that there's anything wrong with not going, I mean," she backtracked, remembering that Allie didn't have a date.

"It's okay, Brooke," Allie smiled. "It's not like there was some guy I was dying to have ask me.

16

I don't want a boyfriend right now anyway — I'm too busy with drama. I'd just like to go because this is the first year that I've really liked school. So I wish I could celebrate that, now that it's almost over. . . ." Allie's voice started to trail off. "Hm. Almost over. Wow."

The three of them got very quiet. They sat for a while, brushing the last of the sugar from their hands and soaking up the hot sun. Both Sean and Brooke were already sunburned and covered with freckles. Allie reached into her bag and slowly pulled on a cotton baseball cap. A skateboarder sailed by, and a breeze rippled the store awnings.

"Boy, it'll be weird not to live in Redwood Hills next year," Sean said finally. The girls were very quiet. They'd all lived their whole lives in the Northern California town, except for the six months of junior year when Allie and her family had lived in New York. "Sometimes I can't believe I'm really graduating, that I'm really going to college."

"I know." Brooke rested her head on his shoulder. Sean would be attending Cal Tech in Southern California, while she'd be at UC Santa Cruz in the north. They'd decided: Those were the best schools for each of them, and it would take more than distance to break them up.

"I can believe it," Allie said. "I'm not sick of high school — actually, this year it's kind of like everything's new. But after what happened when I was a junior, I think it'll be good to go someplace new, you know, have a fresh start."

"Do you wish you were going away, that you

17

could move away from home, too?" Sean asked Allie. Even though her grades weren't great, her professor father had gotten her into nearby Redwood College. The big discussion was whether her protective parents would let her move into the dorms or make her live at home.

"Maybe I won't have to deal with that."

"Huh?"

Allie suddenly glanced up and down the walkway as if someone were after her. She tipped her face back up to Sean and Brooke. "Maybe, just maybe, I won't go to Redwood College at all."

"What!"

"If I'm really lucky, that is."

"Al, what are you talking about!"

Allie looked around again and gestured for Sean and Brooke to climb down onto the back of the bench next to her. When they were both sitting close, Allie whispered, "I've been dying to tell you guys, but I was afraid to say it over the phone, and there was never the right time at school. So, well, here goes. I auditioned for this really good acting school in San Francisco."

Brooke's big eyes got even bigger. "You mean it's not a regular college?"

Allie shook her head. "It's just for actors — they call it a professional training program. It's connected with the theater we went to junior year — on that field trip."

"Your parents will have a fit. They'll never let you go."

"I know. But I probably won't get accepted. They only take fifteen students a year. That's why I didn't tell my parents. If I don't get in, which I probably won't, what's the point of starting a big thing?"

"Al, what if you do get in?"

"Then I'll be so ecstatic, I'll just take it from there. Anyway, I'll wait and see. Probably I'll end up studying English at Redwood College like my dad wants me to and living at home."

They grew silent again. Brooke nestled against Sean. Allie leaned her chin on her hands and stared down the mall. They sat like that while more shoppers flooded the sidewalks, and the sun moved a few inches farther over the roof of the Bubble Café. Finally Brooke popped to her feet and pulled Allie up with her.

"Come on, Al. We'd better go look for this dress before I totally lose my nerve."

Allie brightened. "Okay. Leave everything to me."

Sean stood up and stretched his long legs. "Hey, Brooke, maybe you should wear that dress you wore to the dance junior year, when we met."

Allie and Brooke faced each other and rolled their eyes. Brooke had this talent for always wearing the wrong thing. Although somehow, when it came to Sean, everything about Brooke was just right. "Forget it, Sean," Allie giggled, dragging Brooke away.

"But I loved that dress."

"Don't worry," Brooke yelled back, "I'm sure I'll pick out something just as bad."

Sean laughed and waved and watched them go — Brooke's confident gait, hands in her overall pockets, flat shoes making a sure, straight line. And Allie, gesturing and dancing around her, her earring and the ruffles on her socks bouncing and fluttering. He watched them for a long time, enjoying the sight of them too much to turn away until they were both out of sight.

Then he bounced on his heels, leaped over a bench, and headed toward Payson's Stereo. He took long, peppy steps, everything inside him bursting with excitement. Graduation. College! The idea of tackling the world, really pushing and testing himself, made him almost giddy. Senior year was the best. His scrawny egghead image was so far in the past that even he barely remembered it. There was finally a reward for being smart, for being different and working hard. He'd been accepted to Cal Tech. His folks were proud, his pals envious. He adored Brooke and had great friends like Allie and Nick and his other buddies at school. Yesterday he'd even been selected as valedictorian. This was the payoff for those painful times when he was picked on and made fun of — times that he would never have to live through again. High on hope and bubbly anticipation, Sean sailed into Payson's.

CHAPTER 3

Celia sang to herself as she made a fresh pot of coffee. No dregs for a college guy like Derek Jamison. She found a mug without a single chip and a doily with the Redwood College emblem. When she passed the silver ice-cream bin, she remembered her mother saying there was nothing better than hot coffee with a dab of vanilla ice cream. Celia dipped and dabbed. This evening she wanted things to be special.

She balanced her tiny tray on the flat of her palm and held it high like those pictures of waitresses from the forties. She swung her hips; she tossed her blonde hair. She wove skillfully across the Redwood College Underground Café passing sorority girls and grad students until she stood next to Derek's table.

Derek was reading. Celia watched him, not wanting to interrupt. Besides, she liked just looking at his pale mustache and his lean, handsome face. She liked his tweed jacket with the suede elbow patches, his faded khakis, and his scuffed loafers. In fact, being around guys like Derek was what she liked most about her part-time waitressing job at the college café.

When Derek didn't notice her, Celia leaned over and blew a puff of air along his neck. The side of his straight hair flopped up, then down again. "I brought you a present."

Derek held up his hand and continued to stare at the books spread out in front of him. He finally finished the page he was reading. "Hi, babe," he said.

Celia slid the coffee under his nose and sat. She watched his face, trying to find an answer in his gray-green eyes. She'd only been dating Derek for a few weeks, so she couldn't read him yet. She had to know if her high school career was going to end in a glorious burst or poop out with a disappointing fizzle.

Derek seemed preoccupied. He checked his watch. "You finished already?"

"I'm off." She leaned her lovely face in her hands and grinned at him. "Well?"

"Well, what?"

"Come on, Derek. You know well what!"

Derek frowned and went back to his reading, absentedmindedly bringing the coffee to his lips. He had this way of ignoring her sometimes that drove Celia crazy, but she figured it was part of his being a college freshman, a future famous poet, and — as of one week ago — a member of Sigma Delta, the best fraternity on campus.

Suddenly Derek threw his head back and made

a face. He slammed the coffee down and dabbed the napkin to his mustache. "What's in this!" he objected. It was as if she'd just given him a mug of caster oil.

"Ice cream."

Derek proved her point by pushing the coffee away. "Celia, coffee is meant to be drunk black."

"Sorry." There was a pause filled with the sounds of dishes clanging, students laughing, and a Jackson Browne song coming from the jukebox. Celia could only hope that Derek's reaction to the coffee was not a hint of things to come. When she couldn't stand it any longer, she blurted, "Derek, did you decide? I have to know. Did you decide if you wanted to go to my prom or not!"

Derek gave her that look again. Sort of thoughtful and spacy, as if he were thinking up an epic poem, rather than reflecting back on whether he was willing to escort her to the most important event of her senior year. At this rate, the tickets would be gone by the time he made up his mind. They were only on sale for two more days.

"Derek, why don't you answer me?"

Derek took out a little spiral notebook and started to scribble. "Give me a second, babe. I just got an idea."

Celia stifled her impulse to scream. She learned patience from her only serious boyfriend, Tim Holt. Tim had required patience because he was so quiet and sensitive. But Tim was very different from Derek. Tim was the kind of boy to fall in love with. Deeply in love. And when things between them had ended the previous summer, it had been hard for Celia to recover. That's why

Celia liked Derek. She sensed that he was the right kind of guy for her now — not silly and loud like high school boys — but sophisticated, mature. And distant enough so that she wouldn't fall for him as she had for Tim. And most important, he would look perfect on her arm at her senior prom.

"So you really want to go to some dumb high school prom?"

"Everyone wants to go to their senior prom, Derek."

"Well." Derek winked and finally put down his pencil. As if he were fishing out a present for a little kid, he began emptying his coat pocket. Out came his pipe, a pouch of tobacco, a schedule of foreign movies on campus, a fountain pen, and a container of Tic Tacs. Finally a small envelope appeared. He leaned back to load his pipe and pushed the envelope toward Celia. "All right. Here."

"What's this?" She tried not to appear too greedy as she tore the envelope open. "Oh, my God! Derek!" she screamed, pulling out the tickets. He shushed her. Nothing could dampen her excitement. Two tickets. The Palace Hotel. Redwood High Prom, Class of '88. Derek had even gone to Redwood to buy the prom tickets himself. Celia flew across the table to embrace him. "I promise you'll have a great time. Honest!"

He returned the tickets to his pocket, kissed her lightly on the lips, and guided her back into her seat. "I'd still rather see that French movie over here that night. It's the only night it's playing."

"Derek, this is my only senior prom."

He drew on his pipe and looked around, as if somebody might be watching, then let the smoke out in little puffs. "As long as it's just this once. I don't make a habit of hanging out with high school kids, you know."

"Don't worry. I don't hang out with many kids from my class anymore, either."

Derek nodded, puffed on his pipe some more, and returned to his reading.

Celia eased back in her chair, feeling more content than she had for weeks. Lately she'd been feeling a little lost, alone. She'd outgrown the kids in her class. Oh, she still was friends with a few girls from the popular crowd. And Meg, of course, since she lived next door. Nick, too — but he was her cousin, so he didn't count. Other than that, Celia was above high school. Certainly she was above hanging out with Allie or Sean and his girl friend Brooke. It was a good thing they had gone their separate ways junior year. That had saved Celia the awful task of having to dump them later on. She didn't miss them. Not at all. Secure in that fact, she resisted dipping a spoon into the ice cream melting in Derek's coffee, and watched him read.

Just then a familiar voice pierced through the music, and Celia's contentment vanished.

"Hi, Cici. I finished my test early. How was work?"

Celia jerked her head up. She saw the tips of frosted hair, the eye shadow that glimmered, and the lipstick that was too bright. Her mother! She was hugging a stack of books, as though she thought she was a regular college student. A professor at the next table stared as she strode over. "Mom, what are you doing here?" Celia whispered desperately. Derek looked up, too.

"I finished my test early and I thought I'd visit you." Before Celia could stop her, her mom noticed the mug with the ice cream. "Mmm. My favorite. Is this yours, Cici? Can I have some?"

"It's Derek's," Celia said pointedly.

"Excuse me," her mom responded in that tone that said she thought Celia was being a jerk. She reached her hand across the table. Her nails were painted fluorescent lavender. "You must be Derek. I'm Mrs. Cavenaugh."

"How do you do," Derek said stiffly, shaking her hand.

Celia cringed. So far she'd been able to hide her mother from Derek. Her mom was going back to school, working toward a degree in business. Sometimes she and Celia drove together, but Celia usually met her in the parking lot so no one would see them. "Mom, I'm done. I'll meet you at the car. Okay?"

Her mother rolled her eyes and tugged at her short skirt. The professor stared again. "Whatever you say, Cici," she said with familiar sarcasm. "See you at the car."

Derek watched her walk away, staring almost as hard as the professor. "Your mom sure looks young," Derek said.

Celia gulped, not sure how to respond. "Yeah. Well. She's kind of weird. I really grew up with my aunt and uncle — you know — Jack Rhodes — he used to be a state senator." Celia looked away, afraid of being caught in her lie. "See, um,

26

my parents divorced when I was eleven, and I've barely seen my dad since then, so. . . ."

As usual, when Celia starting talking about herself, Derek lost interest. He was bent over his little notebook again, alternately staring off, then scribbling and doodling.

Luckily, before Celia rambled on any further, they had new visitors. A swarm of tall, hunky young men surrounded the table. They all looked at least nineteen or twenty years old and wore identical Sigma frat pins on their starched collars. Derek put away his notebook and relit his pipe. Now he was all attention. So was Celia.

"How's our newest frat brother?" teased the oldest-looking guy as he leaned over the table. He was very tan and wore a Redwood College letter sweater. He punched Derek's arm and laughed. "Didn't catch a cold, did you?"

Derek shrugged and tittered. "No, Bruce. I'm fine."

Bruce crouched down next to Celia. "You should have seen Jamison on pledge night," he told her, pointing at Derek, "running across the commons in his birthday suit."

"What!" Celia knew that guys did just about anything when they pledged fraternities, but she couldn't imagine Derek doing anything as childish as racing across campus stark naked. Derek didn't seem embarrassed, though. He was looking up at his frat brothers, smiling proudly.

Bruce took a step back and looked Celia up and down. She blushed. "Wow, she's a looker." He jabbed Derek with his elbow. "You better bring her to the big open house next month."

27

"Okay," Derek grinned.

Bruce was still staring at Celia. He leaned in. "So, you live in Stevenson?"

"Are you talking to me?" Celia wanted to introduce herself, but no one seemed interested in learning her name.

"Yeah. Stevenson Hall. Bradley? McClain?"

Celia realized that Bruce was referring to the on-campus dorms. He'd taken her for a college student.

Bruce didn't wait for an answer. "Derek, I'm telling you, you have to bring this gorgeous girl. Even though you're not a pledge anymore, you still have to do what we say." Bruce loomed over Celia again. "You wouldn't want to miss it, would you? Party of the year?"

"No way," Celia giggled. "Just as long as it's not the same night as my senior pr — " Derek's foot stomped hers under the table and Celia gasped in pain. Even though Derek wasn't looking at her, she knew it was a signal. But it wasn't until she glanced toward the doorway that she realized what he was trying to tell her.

Her mother! Her mom hadn't left at all but was standing and chatting with that professor, sipping a mug of coffee and waving wildly for Celia to hurry up. People were staring. Celia prayed that Bruce hadn't seen her. It was bad enough that Derek was so embarrassed. She shoved back her chair, almost plowing into Bruce and another frat brother, wriggled between them, and started for the door.

"What's the matter?" Bruce guffawed, "Did we

shock you, telling you about Jamison running around naked? Can't take it that the guy you're sitting with is a pervert?" They all laughed so hard that everyone in the café stared. The laughter echoed inside Celia's head.

"I just have to go," she called weakly, not acknowledging her mother as she rushed past her. " 'Bye, Derek."

Celia scurried out onto the concrete walk. It was dry and still hot. Students strolled lazily and the trees cast long shadows. Celia headed for the commons. She was followed by the clatter of high heels on concrete — her mom running after her, trying to catch up.

"Cici, wait up. What's your hurry!"

Celia strode faster.

"All right, don't wait for me," her mother huffed in frustration. "I'll meet you at the car."

Celia pretended not to hear. She jogged off the walkway, across the lawn, past the student union and the sculpture garden until she reached the parking lot. The laughter was still ringing in her head, and she was starting to get this funny feeling again, the one she'd been getting all through senior year. It felt like she was swimming and trying to touch the bottom. She'd reach down further and further, stretching and straining, but there was nothing solid there. The nothingness went on forever.

She shot across the parking lot and found their ancient Datsun. It had rust around the doors and a HONK IF YOU LOVE YOUR HAIRDRESSER bumper sticker.

A few minutes later her mother arrived, panting. "Well, get in. It's open," her mom said, now out-and-out angry.

Celia looked around to make sure that no one was watching and climbed in the car. As she got in, she ignored her mother and faced the door. All this would pass, she told herself. The weird feeling, the laughter, the Datsun that smelled like old shoes. She was going to the prom with a terrific guy, a great-looking college guy. And even her humiliating mother couldn't take that away from her.

CHAPTER 4

Run....

Run as hard as you can for as long as you can. No time to plan or maneuver, worry or think. Just run, Meg told herself. Run! Her legs pounded the track. Another turn in the oval length of cinder, and she'd be at the finish line. She could hear the eager screams telling her that she was getting close.

"THAT'S IT. GO, MEG!"

Patrick's voice, sweet and high and excited. More excited than she was because all she felt now was pure motion. Stride, stride, stride. Her shoes meeting the track as though she were on a conveyor belt. Her body and her mind separated from the rest of the world by her speed and her concentration. The other girls huffing, their feet slapping the cinder around her. Some trying to catch up, others trying to jostle their way out of the pack. Only two ahead of Meg and both probably worring about who had the most saved up for the last hundred yards.

Meg ran harder.

The track straightened out and the finish line was in sight. Meg tried to go into her kick even though her lungs were already raw and her legs were screaming. Up on her toes, arms tucked, head down and a little forward. Everything else a blur — the crowd, the sky, the Redwood High coach, the other competitors vaulting and jumping in the middle of the field.

But suddenly her legs went leaden. She'd been running all out the whole way. Still fifty yards to the finish line and she was falling back. The air burned as she sucked it in. The harder she pushed the less speed she seemed to pick up. She strained. She struggled. A girl in maroon Cotter High shorts eased by her on the inside. Two on her own team shot past her on the right.

And then it was a whirr of applause and shouts, elbows and silky running shorts. Meg in the middle of the pack now, her foot over the line amid so many other Nikes and Adidas and Pumas. Too many. She'd finished eighth, maybe ninth. Who knew how many girls had whizzed by her in the last few yards. Meg pulled up, completely winded, and wondered what it was that had made her run like that.

She cleared the way for the last runners and squinted into the stands. Now she saw clearly. Every bleacher. Every face. But she didn't see Patrick. And she didn't see Nick. She stood there until old Miss Snyder, the running coach, yelled at her to keep moving. Meg moved.

"All right, Meg, great race."

Patrick's voice again. Who else would be so kind as to compliment her on a race like that? But he sounded close. Meg looked to the stands again. Then she saw him. For some reason he was on the field, inside the track. He was loping toward her, grinning and clapping his hands. When he reached her he gave her a congratulatory pat.

"Ugh, did I blow that one," Meg grumbled, still cooling down along the inside lane.

"No, you didn't." Patrick ambled beside her on the grass.

She wiped her long dark hair away from her face and watched their legs. His cowboy boot. Her track shoe. His loose easy gait. Her angry stride. His soft jeans. Her hard tan legs, dusty and pinkish from the run. "I went out way too fast."

"I thought you were great."

"That was so dumb. I know better than that!"

"It's okay, Meg."

"I should have come in third, fourth, at least."

"Meg, it's only a track meet."

There was applause from the Cotter crowd as someone vaulted, sailed, and bounced. Patrick turned back to watch. His blue eyes were sweet and clear and the breeze was tossing his long hair across his face. When he caught Meg looking at him, he grinned again and bounced a few times on the heels of his boots.

Meg took a big breath as she realized that she was taking her frustration out on Patrick. He was the last person to deserve it. "You're right. I'm

33

sorry." They walked on together, and he put his arm around her. "I'm pretty gross and sweaty."

"Yeah, but you have great legs."

Meg smiled. "Hey, what are you doing down on the field?" She wasn't sure why she asked. As vice-president Patrick was allowed to go most everywhere, but he usually watched her races from the stands. He gave her that grin again — a little sly, excited, unlike the usual calm, serious Patrick. When he didn't answer her question, she playfully poked his stomach. "You're in a good mood."

"Yup."

The runners were lining up for the next race. Meg and Patrick skirted to the outside of the track. "Any special reason?"

"Yup."

"Are you going to tell me what it is?"

"Maybe."

"Patrick."

He opened the wire fence and nodded toward the stands. "I'll race you to the top bleacher."

"No fair. I just finished a race."

He touched her damp cheek. "It's the only way I can win."

She laughed. "How about if I meet you up there?"

"I'll take you any way I can."

She collected her warm-up suit, then stretched her calves while Patrick climbed ahead of her, his long legs taking two benches at a time. By the time she had her sweats on and her jacket tied around her waist, he was up on top, looking down and still grinning.

Meg hesitated, pretending to take one more stretch. Instead she looked into the stands again. Just like before the race. That was when her brain went crazy — searching, examining, thinking. She'd see Sean and Brooke sometimes. Allie, too. They'd carry on and wave when she glanced up at them. Once she thought she'd seen Celia.

And Nick. Nick was always there, pen and newspaper notepad in hand, his chin leaning on his fist, his golden hair reflecting the afternoon sun. Meg had seen him today. Maybe that was why she ran so stupidly. Whenever she saw Nick she thought about the way things used to be until she was so confused that she had to run like crazy, run so there was no energy left to think about Nick or Patrick or herself. Meg couldn't help looking into the bleachers one more time. Nick was gone now. Just like he was always gone by the time her race ended. She climbed up the benches to join Patrick.

"Looking for somebody?" Patrick asked when she folded down next to him.

"Just seeing who's here."

"Not the greatest turnout." It wasn't an important meet, so the stands were less than half full. There wasn't a soul in the ten or so rows below them. Patrick gazed at her. "You ready for my news?"

"I'm always ready for good news."

"What do you want first? The good news or the great news?"

"There's both?"

That grin again. "There's both."

"Patrick, what!"

35

Patrick pulled a folded white paper out of his pocket and inched closer. "I happen to have a sneak preview of the prom queen nominations."

"How'd you get that? It's not supposed to be announced until tomorrow."

"I have ways." He nudged her and laughed. "Meyer left them sitting on her desk when I got her to sign that acid rain petition." Meg pinched the paper from him, but he stole it back. "But you're much too honest to look."

"I am?" she bubbled. It wasn't really that important to her. Things like winning homecoming queen or cheerleader didn't seem to matter much now that they were seniors. Still, it was fun. Meg sat very still, then tried to grab the paper again.

"Well, if you want to know that badly." Patrick slowly opened it, hiding the contents from her. "Hmm. I see Rebecca Steinmetz's name."

"Of course."

"Maria Martinez."

"Ditto."

"Jessica Westerheim." Patrick paused for some patchy applause at the end of the four-forty. "I can't quite read this last one. Peg McCoo? Mugs Magrew? Mr. Magoo? No, I think it looks like Meg McCall."

"Must be a mistake."

"Look for yourself."

Meg giggled. "Wow." Suddenly she fretted. "Is that the whole list?"

"That's all four."

"Oh. Not Celia?"

Patrick looked a little let down that Meg wasn't

more excited. "Nope. I guess people think she's too removed from things this year."

Meg knew that was true. She also knew that even though Celia acted bored with high school, she'd be disappointed. "That's great though. How about king?"

Patrick grinned again. "Nick Rhodes. Jim Burke. Bob Barnett. And yours truly."

"You! Oh, Patrick." She gave him a quick hug, then pulled back. "So, is that the great news, too?" she wondered. She couldn't imagine sensible Patrick making that big a deal out of prom king.

Patrick folded the paper and slipped it back in his pocket. His grin was gone. "No. There's more."

"What else?"

He took her hand and stared at it for a long time, as if he were reading her fortune.

"Patrick," Meg prompted softly, "what is it?"

Patrick sat up and looked around. "Uh, it's a little more involved. How about we go out and celebrate the first news, and then I'll tell you the rest. Because the second news . . . well, the second news is great but in some ways not great and sort of confusing and I think we should talk about it."

Meg turned to face him and brushed his long hair away from his eyes. "What is it?"

"I need the right setting. I figured over a long evening of candlelight and a giant plate of onion rings at the Bubble Café. How about it? We could even order two plates of onion rings."

"Patrick, I can't go out tonight," Meg said after a pause. "I have that chem quiz tomorrow. Plus I have to write the grad night announcement and pick up my shoes for the prom." He looked much more disappointed than she'd expected. She bumped him with her elbow, trying to make his grin reappear. "Why can't you tell me here?"

"I don't know." Patrick turned away. They sat quietly, staring at the last few events, not really watching. Finally the meet ended and the crowd started to filter down. From where Meg and Patrick sat they could see the cars lining up at the parking lot exit and the Cotter High buses puffing clouds of gray exhaust. Patrick finally got up and slowly climbed down the bleachers. Meg followed.

By the time they got into his old station wagon Patrick had grown silent and glum. He put a James Taylor tape in the stereo, tossed some old blankets and leaflets and tools in the back, and drove Meg home. James Taylor was still singing and playing a sad guitar when they arrived.

Patrick didn't turn the motor off when he pulled over in front of her house. Meg made no move toward the door. Instead, she touched his arm. "Patrick, are you going to tell me? Considering that you have great news, you sure are acting gloomy all of a sudden."

He shrugged.

She leaned closer. "At this rate, I'd hate to see how you'd act if you won the state lottery."

He smiled in spite of himself, then suddenly he said, "I got into Cornell."

"What?"

"Cornell University. They accepted me."

"When did you find out?"

"The letter came today. I guess my number on the waiting list came up. I called home before the meet and my dad told me."

"Oh, Patrick, that is great!" Meg threw herself against him, her arms encircling his slim shoulders, her long hair mingling with his. He immediately responded, clutching her so tightly she could hardly breathe. Then he went limp. Meg pulled back. "Why aren't you more excited? It's the perfect college for you."

Patrick held up his hands. "I haven't decided yet what I'm going to do. I might still stay here and go to Berkeley."

"But Cornell is where you really want to go."

"I know."

"At least now you can decide between the two. Patrick, it's great!" Meg didn't say any more. They'd been through this before, and it always stopped at an awkward point. Because Meg didn't want to hurt Patrick. Because neither of them knew quite what to say.

It had started when Meg decided on the University of California at Berkeley, which was about two hours from Redwood Hills, near San Francisco. For years Patrick had dreamed of studying soil science at Cornell, which was all the way across the country in upstate New York. But when he heard about Meg's choice, he applied to Berkeley, too. He pretended that it was just in case Cornell rejected him, but then he sent his Cornell application in late — intentionally, Meg suspected. So, he ended up with an acceptance to

Berkeley, while only being wait-listed for Cornell.

"I have to think about it," he said defensively. "You know Berkeley is a really good school, too."

"I know."

"And it's cheaper."

"Yes."

"And a lot closer to my family. I could wait and go to Cornell for graduate school."

"You could."

"I don't have to decide right now."

"Still, it's great that they want you, Patrick. Cornell is the best school for what you want to study. Aren't you excited about that?"

"Sure. It's just . . . you know."

Meg took a deep breath. Finally, she said it. "Patrick lots of couples go to different colleges. Look at Sean and Brooke."

"I know. It's just. . . ." He closed his eyes as if he couldn't bear to say any more. Suddenly he pulled her toward him. "I guess it's that. . . ." He kissed her. A long, sweet kiss. Then he buried his face against her neck. "I love you," Meg heard him whisper.

Everything inside Meg clamped down. They had both stopped breathing for a moment, and she knew that Patrick was waiting to see if she'd say it, too. They both sat there, listening to their hearts pound. Meg's mind was going like crazy again.

"Oh, Patrick," she finally whispered. Her brain wouldn't stop now — figuring, worrying, searching. She suddenly wished she could be back at the track running or jumping until she was blank with exhaustion. She turned to Patrick. "Listen, are you still in the mood to go out? You know what a sucker I am for onion rings."

"I thought you had to study."

"I guess I could do it in the morning. And I guess my shoes and the other stuff can wait one more day."

"Okay." He leaned forward to finally turn off the engine, then reconsidered. "Do you need time to change? I could go home and come back."

Meg turned the stereo up until it blared, then quickly kissed him and jumped out. "No. I'll be back out here and ready by the time this song is over." She leaped up the front steps, vaulted over the porch swing, and ran as fast as she could through her front door.

CHAPTER
5

Allie sat outside her father's classroom at Redwood College and watched the young man watch her. She'd been sitting there for almost an hour — since the bus had dropped her off after school — and for almost that entire hour the young man had gawked and gazed at her.

Allie giggled. The more the boy stared, the more she leaned back, posing, playing a part. She couldn't help it. She felt beautiful. Special. Talented and exotic. It was one of the rare moments in her life when she felt that Allie Simon was exactly the right person to be.

"Hi, babe," the young man said, finally approaching. He was trying to maintain a cool posture, but he was having trouble balancing his leather briefcase and a huge load of books. The pencil wedged behind his ear looked like it was about to color in his scraggly blonde mustache.

He was very handsome, but in her current

mood, Allie couldn't help smirking at him. "Babe? The only Babe I know is Babe Ruth." She glanced down the college hallway at the soda machine and the bulletin boards. "And I don't see him here." She giggled again, so loudly that she was surprised when he sat on the floor next to her and unloaded his books.

He took a pipe out of his pocket and lit it, gesturing toward her father's classroom door as he flicked out the match. "Do you have killer Simon for linguistics? He's a pain."

"You're telling me." Allie stifled another laugh and waved the smoke away with her hand.

He smiled as if he thought she was encouraging him. "You don't mind if I sit here, do you?"

She shrugged.

"You don't look too busy. I thought you might want company."

"It's a free hallway," Allie tossed back, then she was surprised she'd bothered. Flirting didn't usually interest her, but today, with her glorious news bursting inside her, she couldn't resist playing and showing herself off a little.

He leaned in to examine the book that rested in her lap. "What are you reading?"

Allie lifted her paperback copy of *Romeo and Juliet*. "Ever heard of it?"

"Very funny." He inched closer. "You know, you remind me of Juliet."

"Must be my eyes like stars." She crossed her eyes and giggled again. "Or my star-crossed eyes."

He laughed. "You must be in Dr. Howard's Shakespeare class."

"Dr. Howard? Never heard of him."

43

"Just reading Shakespeare for pleasure? Hmm. I like that in a girl."

"Do you?"

"Well, I'm a poet, you see."

"Oh, well, I'm an actress, you see. I'm memorizing Juliet's potion speech. I'm doing it for my final project."

"You must be Acting 1C then. Mr. Cohen? I've heard he's a great prof."

Allie let her laugh go this time, and it bounced off the white ceiling and the shiny linoleum. "Prof? How about Ms. Smith, plain old drama teacher at Redwood High School."

The young man's face fell. The pipe almost fell, too, but he caught it in time and took a puff. "Oh, you're still in high school." He gave the floor a light whap with his palm. "What are you doing here, then?"

Allie gestured toward the door. "Waiting to talk to my dad."

"Your dad?"

"Killer Simon. The pain."

The boy's face reddened, and he tried to take one more puff, but his pipe had gone out. Finally, he tapped it against his palm and stuffed it in the pocket of his tweed jacket. "My name's Derek Jamison," he told her, holding out his hand to shake.

"Allie. Allie Simon."

"So, he's really your dad? Simon?" Allie nodded. "I didn't mean anything, about him being a pain. I just mean he's hard . . . tough grader. All good teachers are tough. You know."

"I know." Allie started to feel more sober as

44

she pictured her father's face and remembered the reason she was waiting to talk to him. She suddenly wished that Brooke and Sean could be with her, although she also knew that this was something she had to do alone. "Believe me, I know." She chewed on her thumbnail and stared at her father's door.

As if Derek could tell that he was losing her attention, he blurted, "Hey, you don't have to talk to your dad this very second, do you?"

"Yes," Allie responded, not taking her eyes off the door. "It's important. Very important."

Derek sorted through his books. "Because I was thinking, a Shakespearean actress like you — you might want to take a look at some of my poems. I'm sending them in to some magazines. I don't let just anybody read them." He held up a small notepad.

"Oh?"

"Yeah. Maybe over at my frat house. Sigma Delta. You've heard of them."

"I don't think so." There was noise behind her father's door now. A chair being pushed back, feet shuffling, and the low hum of voices. Allie sat up. Her stomach became a hard, tight ball, and her skin was damp.

Derek waved his notepad. "It's the best frat on campus. Not just jocks, either. Smart, artistic guys like me."

"That's nice." The classroom door squeaked opened and people started to file out. They were older, probably grad students. Allie shot to her feet and stared at her sparkly belt and lace-up sandals. She should have worn something more conservative — something that made her look more responsible and mature.

"Well, I guess if this isn't a good time to show you my poems, maybe I should give you a call," Derek rambled.

Derek's voice had become part of the background noise that now rumbled down the hallway. He made as much of an impression on Allie as the thunk of the soda can dropping into the dispenser of the Coke machine. She was only fully aware of her father, whom she watched through the doorway. He was cleaning his glasses with a handkerchief and examining a diagram he'd written on the blackboard.

Derek had removed the pencil from behind his ear and had it poised over the cover of his notepad. "So what did you say your phone number was?"

"I didn't."

He laughed. "Oh, yeah. Are you in the book?"

"Unlisted." Allie stood at the door frame until the last of her father's students left. It was time. Her breath was short, and her stomach was bouncing around like a pinball. Derek had completely faded, even though he seemed to be practically yelling and waving his hand for her attention.

"Oh. You going to make me work for it?" he continued with a forced smile. "Playing hard to get, huh. You know, Juliet didn't do that."

"Excuse me, I have to talk to my dad."

"It's okay. I can find you. Allie Simon, Redwood High."

"I have to go."

"Wait! It'll be a lot easier if you just give me your phone. . . ."

She barely noticed Derek slap his arms against his thighs and give the wall a light punch. Then he was gone, because Allie was inside her father's classroom. She slowly shut the door. Her father was erasing the board, and she watched his bald spot bob up and down as he swept the board clean. The room was so quiet that Allie could hear the hum of the air conditioner and the pounding of her heart. "Hi, Daddy."

He turned around, surprised. "Al, what are you doing here?" he asked pleasantly.

Allie walked up to a front desk and sat. Her father was smiling with affection. Still, he had one cautious eyebrow raised as if he had to watch her, or she'd pull a lamp down on her head or stick a hairpin in an electric socket.

Suddenly it didn't seem real anymore. Allie pulled the manila envelope out of her book bag to prove to herself that she hadn't imagined it. She was grown up. She'd done it, on her own. Her father went on tidying his room as she opened her envelope and pulled out the contents. She read over the letter, even though she'd read it fifty times already.

Dear Allie Simon,

We are pleased to inform you that you have been accepted to the professional actors' training program of the San Francisco Conservatory Theater beginning in the fall of 1988.

Congratulations.

There were other papers and cards. She'd known when she'd seen it waiting for her in the mailbox that it said yes. Everybody said that a fat packet meant yes. A slim letter probably meant no. Her envelope was bursting with postcards and forms to be filled out and sent back.

Allie set her acceptance letter on the edge of the desk, as if it were a completed pop quiz. She'd rehearsed a speech for this moment, but the opening line would not come to her.

"What's that paper, Al?" her father asked, dusting his hands and letting off little clouds of chalk. He picked up the letter and slowly read it.

She watched his affectionate smile tighten into pale, pursed lips. His bald spot turned crimson and a vein started to throb in his forehead. He whipped off his glasses. "What is this supposed to mean!"

Allie cleared her throat, praying that something like a voice would come out. "Uh, it means they thought I was good enough." A little of what she had planned to say was coming back to her. "The San Francisco Acting Conservatory. I got accepted."

He didn't hand the letter back. "So I see," Mr. Simon said, clearing his throat. "When did you apply for this" — he paused and read the letter again — "training program?" He said those two words as if they were the same as "reform school."

"I didn't just apply. I auditioned."

"Without telling me or your mother?"

Allie swallowed. Her mouth was getting so dry

48

that it was hard to speak. "Um, I wrote to them last fall and sent for an application. Then I worked on two audition pieces with my drama teacher, and I went to San Francisco over spring break for the audition. Penny and Richard, two other kids from my class, went with me."

"Was that the day you said you were going to Fisherman's Wharf?"

"Yes."

"So you lied about where you were going."

"No, I mean, we went to Fisherman's Wharf. We just went to the audition first." Her father took off his glasses and shook his head disgustedly. "Penny and Richard auditioned, too. I'm the only one who got accepted."

"That's nice," her father spat out sarcastically. He stood staring at her with his arms folded, as if she'd just told him she was quitting school to join the circus or live on the streets. "That is just lovely."

"Daddy!" Allie stood up and pounded the desktop with her fist. Her father's cynicism made tears fly down her cheeks. All the old feelings surged back — the frustration, the hopelessness, the feeling that Allie Simon was destined to be a worthless nothing. "Why can't you be proud of me for getting in?" she cried. "Finally, I do something right, really right, and all you do is make fun of me and act like it's not important. It's not fair!"

Her father leaned back against the board and watched her cry. "What's this? Are you trying to show me what a good actress you are?"

Allie's rage swelled. "I'm not acting! I'm upset! This is really important to me, don't you realize that?"

"I realize that you are too emotional about this right now to make an intelligent decision."

"I made an intelligent decision. I did it on my own and I succeeded. But you won't see — "

"Allie," he cut her off, "I don't think you are mature enough to decide rationally about your future. I think you proved that last year."

Allie pushed her tears aside and tried her best to speak clearly. "Daddy, that was last year. I'm a senior now. I'm not a baby anymore. I've learned some things about what I want and what I don't want."

"And I suppose you don't want to go to college. That's the intelligent, mature decision you're telling me you've come to?"

"The training program is like college. It's the kind of college I should go to. Daddy, acting is what I'm good at. I've never been very good in a regular school. If you didn't teach here, they never would have accepted me." Just as Allie thought she was regaining control, her tears exploded again. "I can't face another four years of failure because I'm not doing what I really want to do and because I have to do things I don't care about."

"And how about after those four years?" her father lectured. He moved toward her, pointing his finger. "What then, Allie? I suppose you're going to support yourself as an actress, like the one out of a hundred other kids out there who has this same stupid dream."

"It's not stupid! And maybe I'll be that one in a hundred. At least I can try. Why are you so quick to say I can't do it?"

"Allie, be realistic. The chance of you ever making a living as an actress is nonexistent." As if he'd said the final word, he turned back to his desk and started stuffing papers in his briefcase.

Allie wanted to run over . . . to scream . . . to take his orderly stack of papers and throw it across the room. But for once she made herself stop, catch her breath, and think. In spite of all the success she'd had senior year she'd allowed herself to hook right back into her old hysteria and despair. That was just what her father expected and just what would prove that he was right. She wiped her tears away and raised her head.

"How do you know anything about what my chances of becoming an actress are?" she responded finally in a low, steady voice. "You've never come to see one of my plays at school. All you ask about is how I'm doing in history, how I like my math teacher. You never ask about my drama class and what I'm doing there. You can't know anything about me or what I can do if you don't know about that."

Her father turned back slowly. "Allie, I'm glad that you found something in drama that helped you adjust to school and be happier with yourself. But I haven't wanted to encourage you for just this reason. Being an actress is not the kind of life I want for you."

"What about what I want for me?"

He snapped his briefcase shut, then held up his

hands and looked at her very sternly. "No, Allie. That's my answer. No. You're going to Redwood College, and I'm not paying to send you to acting school. Not one cent. Case closed. End of discussion." There was a long pause as the clock ticked and the air conditioner kicked off. He packed up his briefcase and sighed. "I'm tired. I'd like to go home. How did you get here?"

"The bus."

"I suppose you'll refuse to ride home with me now?"

She hesitated. "No. I'll ride home with you. I'm not a baby."

She waited silently at the door while he finished neatening up and turned out the lights. By the time he joined her in the hall, she had started to figure things out. In a calm voice she told him, "Daddy, if you don't want to send me to acting school, that's fine. I'll get a job and support myself." She held her head higher. She wasn't sure how to go about doing something like this, but she knew she could find out. There had to be other kids whose parents refused to help them or ones whose folks simply couldn't afford it. She'd find out what those kids did and do the same. She'd start tomorrow. "I can do it without your help," she announced. "You wait and see. I'll do it on my own."

Her father didn't say one word as he walked beside her, but his mouth grew pale, and his bald spot stayed very red. Allie could only hope.

CHAPTER 6

GOOD-BYE REDWOOD HIGH. . . .
"Boring."
REDWOOD IS DEADWOOD. . . .
"Too negative."
I'*m* READY AND WOOD LIKE TO GO. . . .
"That's just dumb."

Nick sighed. He was trying to write the very last
piece he'd ever do for the newspaper, but he was
having trouble getting past the title. He was supposed to do an editorial on what it felt like to be
a senior . . . what it meant to be leaving the
school where he'd been part of the first freshman
class. It gave Nick a lump in his throat just thinking about it. That, unfortunately, could not be
featured in the newspaper.

IS THIS WHAT THEY MEAN BY WRITER'S BLOCK?
he finally ended up pounding out on the old
typewriter. He banged the carriage home and
shook his head.

"That's a productive start," he muttered.

Nick usually liked writing for the newspaper. In fact he loved writing now and he knew it. Even the feel of the keys on his old typewriter was cool. Nick could use his dad's computer if he wanted, but he preferred this — an old green Remington from the fifties. It weighed about two tons, so much that Nick's mom had protested that it was a hazard on Nick's desk. What if Hughie knocked it over, she'd warned. What a laugh. Hughie couldn't knock over this hunk with a bulldozer.

Nick leaned back in his chair and stared at the semi-blank page. He bit into a pencil. Usually he just had to report, to relay information. This piece had to come from his heart and his imagination. But whenever he imagined graduation, that lump in his throat just got worse, and Nick didn't think he could write about a lump, even if he wanted to. He didn't know why he should feel like this. His future looked great. He was graduating in the top tenth of his class. He had been accepted at UC Berkeley, and he'd even been invited to try out for the freshman football team. He had nowhere to look but forward.

"I DON'T THINK I CAN TAKE THIS ANYMORE."

"I THOUGHT WE'D DECIDED. WE'RE GOING TO WAIT AT LEAST UNTIL NICK GRADUATES."

"ALL RIGHT. KEEP YOUR VOICE DOWN."

"YOU KEEP YOUR VOICE. . . ."

Nick dug his nails into the side of his typewriter. His parents were fighting again. The lump in his throat got worse. He tried to ease it away by humming to himself. He also hoped that might block out his parents' screeching.

"AS FAR AS I'M CONCERNED, YOU CAN DO WHATEVER YOU WANT."

"LOOK, I DON'T LIKE THIS ARRANGE-MENT ANY BETTER THAN YOU. . . ."

Nick randomly banged the typewriter keys. When that didn't work, he got up from his chair and slammed his door as loudly as he could.

It was quiet for a few minutes, and then they started again, more softly this time.

"Nick heard you."

"Heard *me*? I suppose it's all my fault?"

"Would you be quiet. Nick is in his room."

"ALL RIGHT!"

"LOWER YOUR VOICE."

"LOWER *YOUR* VOICE!!!"

"Lower your voice," Nick scoffed. That was like telling an elephant herd to do a ballet on tiptoes. His parents were arguing so much these days that it was like being in the middle of a perpetual summer thunderstorm — disruptive, frightening, and not a thing in the world Nick could do to stop it. The only way to fight back was to make noise of his own — blare the stereo or the TV, bang dishes, bash pots and pans. Lately he'd even taken to running the bathroom faucet full blast.

He considered going down the hall and talking to them. But when he tried that they turned into mannequin people, all pasted-on smiles and un-natural movements. Sean had witnessed it over spring break and jokingly called them The Stepford Parents, after some horror movie where people turned into androids. But Nick was just as bad. He'd respond to them like he was Harpo Marx — mutely kicking the cabinets or pitching his clothes down the laundry chute as if he were throwing javelins or bombs.

Nick sat back at his desk, but even before his fingers touched the keys he knew it was futile. His brain couldn't work when his head was pounding like this. Now he heard his mother's sensible shoes clip along the hall toward his brother's old room, while his father's wingtips paced their bedroom floor. Nick didn't even want to see his parents faces tonight, those guilty, embarrassed, am-I-pulling-off-the-act? looks.

"I'm gone," Nick whispered to himself. He grabbed a clean shirt, underwear, and writing pad and stuffed it all into a knapsack before he went to the bathroom to get his toothbrush and razor. Finally he went back to the typewriter, where he rolled in a sheet of paper. Inside he felt tight as a drum. Why were his parents trying to hide this from him? Why couldn't they just get it out in the open? He found himself pounding out his note on the typewriter. Each time he hit a key it was like a hammer falling.

G.O.I.N.G . . . T.O . . . C.E.L.I.A'S, Nick pounded. W.I.L.L . . . S.T.A.Y . . . T.H.E.R.E . . . T.O.N.I.G.H.T.

He ripped it out of the typewriter, grabbed his stuff, and rushed downstairs, where he dropped the note on the kitchen table and then left the house.

Outside it was dark but still warm, and there were bugs bopping around the lights that shone down on the driveway. As Nick got in his green Rabbit, he could see Allie's house lit up next door, across the apple orchard. Hughie started to bark and trot over when Nick started the engine, but Nick pulled out before Hughie could reach him. Mindlessly, Nick drove away from the big houses and the ranches and vineyards, until he passed Redwood High and turned into the orderly, crowded neighborhood near downtown. When he pulled up in front of Celia's house, he heard only the squeal of his brakes and a few crickets. He grabbed his knapsack and went up to the front door.

"Cici? Aunt Jody! Hello? Anybody home?" Nick opened the screen door and knocked some more. He tried to peek in the living room window but the drapes were closed, and it seemed like only the porch light was on. He put his knapsack down on the weird sheet of Astroturf that covered the front stoop and dug in the flower bed for the extra key, just like when he was a kid and his folks were away campaigning. Finally he uncovered the old aspirin tin, took out the key, and let himself in.

The living room smelled the same as when he was little — a combination of dust, hair spray, and baking. Celia complained endlessly about this little old house, but Nick liked it. He liked the knitted afghans that were always tossed over the sofa bed and the way his aunt made showy flower arrangements in wine carafes or juice jars. It was sure different from his house, which usually smelled like furniture polish and had those vacuum cleaner tracks on the rugs after the cleaning lady came three times a week.

Nick clicked on two lamps, took out his pad and pencil, kicked off his court shoes, and curled up on the sofa bed. Hoping to get something done on his article, he sat very still. It was peaceful. Quiet. After a few minutes an opening line for his story was beginning to jell in his head.

There was a loud knock on the screen door.

"Great." Nick cursed, startled and annoyed at the interruption. Of course, he could hardly expect Celia and his aunt to stay away so he could use their living room as an office. He trudged across the shag carpet and wondered why he hadn't heard the car pull up or seen the headlights through the drapes. He opened the door.

It wasn't Celia. Or her mother. It was Meg.

"Hi."

"Oh. Hi."

Her hair was pulled back in a sloppy ponytail, but she was holding a fancy dress, covered in plastic, against her torso. She made Nick think of those cut-out cardboard statues at amusement parks where you took a picture of somebody's face over the body of Snow White or Cinderella.

Meg stepped back when he pushed the screen door open. Her dress rustled and crunched. He stared into her blue eyes for what seemed like ages. How long had it been since he and Meg were together, alone, he found himself wondering. How long?

Meg didn't say a word. She just stared back and clutched her dress more tightly.

"Hi," Nick whispered again, finally.

"Is Celia here?"

"Celia?" His brain had gone blank. All he

58

could take in was Meg's eyes and her mouth and the wisps of dark hair streaming down the sides of her face.

She tried to look past him, but he sensed that it was only an excuse not to meet his gaze. "I wanted to show her my dress. For the prom."

"She's not home."

"What are you doing here?"

Nick hesitated. He wasn't sure how much to say. He hadn't told any of his friends about what was going on at home, not even Sean. He had the feeling that if he got started talking about it, he might never be able to stop. "Working on an article for the paper." Meg looked confused. "My room's being painted at home," he heard himself lie. "So I came here instead."

Meg didn't seem convinced. Still, she didn't pursue it. "Do you know when Cici's getting back?"

It was as if they were total strangers, rather than two people who'd spent half their lives together, practically thinking as one. "No. I just got here and let myself in."

Meg backed up. More rustling and crunching. "Well. I guess, oh, tell her to call me. She wanted me to see her prom dress, too." Nick was leaning out, still holding open the screen door. She had backed all the way to the edge of the Astroturf. "Okay?"

"Okay."

She stopped. "I'll be at home." She gestured to her house next door, as if he didn't know where she lived.

Nick could see her parents through the kitchen

59

window, past the potted plants and the porch swing. They were doing the dishes and laughing. That was when Nick flashed back to the last time he and Meg were really alone together. Over a year ago. In the woods behind his house. They were looking for Allie. Meg fell asleep in his arms, and he'd watched her sleeping and thought how he'd never loved anybody as much as he loved her. He suddenly looked away, afraid that his thoughts were going to burst out and Meg would read them all over his face.

She was still standing on the walkway. She hadn't budged. "Nick, are you okay?"

"Sure." Nick forced himself to smile. "If you want, you can come in and wait. I'm sure Celia will be home soon. She's got to be off work by now."

"I don't want to interrupt you or anything."

"It's okay."

"Are you sure?"

"It's fine."

"Honest?"

Nick swallowed hard. "Honest."

"Okay. I guess." When she entered the house they each did an awkward little dance to get out of the other's way. Meg carefully laid her dress over the TV. She started to sit on the sofa, but when Nick sat there, she moved to the easy chair instead.

"So that's your prom dress?"

"Uh-huh. Do you think it's okay?"

Nick shrugged. The way it was slung over the TV it just looked like a sheet of plastic-covered blue. "I'm sure Patrick'll like it."

60

"Are you going?" Meg seemed nervous, crossing and recrossing her legs. She was wearing running shorts and an old sweat shirt. Her feet were bare. "What a dumb question. Of course you're going. You're nominated for prom king."

"I bought a ticket." Nick suddenly got the feeling that she wanted to know who he was going with. He hadn't asked anybody. There was no one he wanted to ask. "I guess I'd better hurry up and find a date. Got any suggestions?" He laughed.

"I'm sure there are plenty of girls who'd give anything to go with you."

"Yeah? Name twelve." She laughed, too. After the laugh ended, it got so quiet that Nick could hear the crickets again. He picked up his notepad and started to doodle. "Sean told me you got accepted premed at Berkeley." She nodded. "Congrats. That's great. I'm going there, too. Journalism major."

"I know. Celia told me."

"Yeah? Its a huge school, but who knows, maybe we'll see each other."

"Maybe."

There was another long silence. Nick continued to doodle until he realized that he had written *Meg McCall Meg McCall Meg McCall*. Quickly, he closed the notepad and slid it under one of the knitted afghans. Then he sat up straight and gazed at her. She looked sad and confused and very beautiful. "I saw your race last week."

"I saw you, too."

"You did?"

"Well, before the race. Not after."

He was surprised that she'd noticed him. "I like

61

to move around the stands, you know, since I'm writing about the meet. I need to see all the events from the best possible places." He would never admit that he liked to sit close to see her run, but always left before he had to watch Patrick swoop her up afterward. "You went out way too fast."

Her head jerked up. For a second she looked shocked, almost insulted. Then she smiled. A full, warm, Meg smile. "Boy, did I ever. That was the worst race I've ever run."

"Why did you run like that?"

"Beats me."

"Not smart."

"I know."

"I thought you were going to pass out or throw up or something, you pushed yourself so hard."

"I almost did."

"That's why I moved away. I didn't want to have to write about that."

"Too gross."

"Much too gross. It would have been like that time in sixth grade when we raced each other up Capitola Mountain right after we'd eaten all of Sean's and Allie's Halloween candy."

"Nick!" Meg brought her hand to her mouth and let out a deep, throaty laugh. "I can't believe you still remember that!"

He looked right at her. "I remember everything."

Meg didn't look away this time. Her expression grew even more confused. But less sad. Suddenly she asked, "Nick, is your room really being painted?"

62

He didn't answer.

Slowly she got up and moved toward him, folding onto the arm of the sofa. Nick stared at the cuff of her sweat shirt and her hand, which was very close to his. She was pulling on the old sofa's loose threads. "You could have worked in another room in your house, couldn't you? I mean, the whole house isn't being painted, is it?"

Nick took a deep breath. He couldn't fool her any more than she could fool him, even after all this time apart. He wanted to tell her about his parents. He sensed that she was the one person he could tell, he should tell. But his mind was too clouded by the nearness of her bare leg. He could feel the warmth from her body and smell something like perfume and salty grass. He turned toward her and the whole world seemed to stop as he moved his hand, so slowly toward her face.

He had barely touched her cheek when the front door flew open.

"Who's in here!"

"Oh, it's just Nick. Hi, Meg."

Aunt Jody and Celia were standing in the doorway. Nick pulled his hand back, and Meg shot to her feet as if she'd been caught in the middle of a burglary. Celia merely smiled and headed for the kitchen, but his aunt stood for a moment, fluffing her tinted hair and staring.

"Hi, Nick, honey. Hi, Meg. What's going on?"

Meg rushed over and scooped up her dress. Her cheeks were scarlet. "Hi, Mrs. Cavenaugh. I just came over to show Cici my prom dress."

"Oh, good!" Celia yelled from the far end of

the kitchen. "Meg, show me! I don't have mine yet. I'm picking it up tomorrow. Derek's going to flip when he sees it. Bring yours in here."

Meg gave Nick and Mrs. Cavenaugh a brief, self-conscious smile, then took her dress into the kitchen.

Celia's mom sat on the arm of the sofa, where Meg had been only a few moments before. Nick threw himself back and clutched a pillow. His arms were trembling and his chest was so tight he could hardly breathe.

"What happened, Nick?" his aunt asked in a soft voice. "Did your folks finally drive you out of the house?"

Nick nodded. He felt the sudden awful pressure of tears and held them back with all his might. His aunt reached over and patted his arm. She was the only person he'd discussed any of this with — mostly because his mother was her sister, and because she'd been through a rough divorce herself. Although, so far, she'd done all the talking. Nick had only listened.

"Are you staying the night, Nick?"

"Can I?"

She gave him a sad smile. "Of course. I'll call your house and make sure your mom knows where you are."

"Thanks."

"Do you want to talk about it, Nick? It'll help. I promise it will."

Nick flinched as Celia squealed with appreciation for Meg's prom dress. "Not now," he whispered. His aunt nodded. They both heard the rustle of plastic and satin as Meg left the kitchen and came back into the living room.

Meg stood for a brief moment in the doorway, glancing quickly at Nick. "I should get home," she said. "Good-night."

"Good-night," Nick and his aunt said at the same time. They watched Meg leave.

Nick sat for a few minutes, listening to Meg's footsteps fade away. Celia was still in the kitchen, noisily fixing herself a snack. His aunt fetched him sheets and blankets.

"You can't hold it all inside forever, Nick," Aunt Jody told him as she dumped a stack of linens on the coffee table.

"I'll be okay." Nick suddenly realized that Celia was standing in the doorway, watching and eating a sandwich.

"Are you sure?"

"Mom, Nick obviously wants to be left alone," Celia interrupted.

A flicker of hurt passed over Mrs. Cavenaugh's face. She brushed her bangs back with a purple fingernail and stood up. "Good-night, kids." She blew Nick a kiss. "Let me know if you need anything."

"Thanks, Aunt Jody. Sleep well."

"You, too, honey."

Celia and Nick were both very still after her mother went into the bathroom and closed the door. The rumble of the shower started, and Celia slumped down next to Nick. She handed him half her sandwich.

"You don't always have to be such a jerk to

your mom," Nick said, after a moment. They ate slowly, distractedly. "She's trying to help."

Celia's blonde hair framed her perfect face, which suddenly looked as sad as Meg's. "I know." She sighed. "It's just . . . oh, never mind." Brushing the crumbs off her hands, she stood and picked up the sheets. "I'll help you make up the bed, okay?"

"Okay." They tugged out the mattress and pulled on the sheets.

"Is stuff weird at home again?" Celia asked when they were finished and stood staring off in different directions.

"I can handle it."

"I remember when my dad was still here. I hated it so much when they yelled at each other. I used to pretend that they weren't really my parents. I'd pretend that I really belonged to your mom and dad."

"That's a laugh," Nick said, not smiling.

"Parents are weird."

"You're telling me."

Suddenly, Celia took a few steps closer. She gave him a tentative pat on the shoulder. Nick immediately pulled her in for a quick hug.

"I thought by the time you were a senior everything was supposed to make sense," Celia said, pulling back.

"Fat chance." Nick gave her arm a mock punch. "Sleep tight."

" 'Night." Celia went to the doorway, then turned back. "Don't let the bedbugs bite."

Nick waited until Celia's door closed before snuggling into bed. He pulled the sheet up, then

66

tugged one of the afghans down and wrapped it around him. As he did something hard and sharp tumbled onto the floor. His notepad. He picked it up and thought about the opening line for his article. He thought about his parents. And he thought about Meg and how he'd written her name that way. Three times. He clutched the notepad to his chest. He fell asleep like that, still holding it.

CHAPTER
7

"You really want a job, Al?"

"I have to get one, Sean."

"Ugh."

"Sean," Brooke stressed, "it's important."

"Get a job, doo, da-doo, doo," Sean sang as he slithered back and forth past the Redwood High flagpole. He was doing a kind of moonwalk, but also something that looked like a piece of spaghetti rolling around. It was after school, so there weren't too many passersby to stop and stare.

"Sean! Don't be a dork," Allie objected. "Just because you know you can work in your parents' bike store all summer."

"Who says that's so great? Pumping tires and cleaning gears?"

"Its better than McDonald's."

"Or Wendy's or Taco Bell," added Brooke.

"You'd think for minimum wage they could at least let you make real food."

Allie plopped down on the curb and flung open *The Redwood Hills Daily*. She looked over the want ads she'd circled in red crayon. Brooke crouched behind her, reading over her shoulder and frowning.

"It might not be so bad," Sean went on. "Think of those hot apple pies and tender strips. And, let's not forget Allie's all-time favorite, Chicken McNuggets!"

Brooke tried to keep frowning, but she finally started to giggle, which of course started Allie giggling, too. Sean smiled, having finally accomplished his mission, which was to make the girls laugh.

"Well," Allie sighed, refolding the newspaper and sticking it in her book bag. "I just have to start looking."

"You'll find something," Brooke encouraged.

"I'm sure you will," Sean added in an overly serious voice. "But believe me, most jobs are highly overrated." Both girls punched him. He grinned.

"Okay. Here I go." Allie stood up and straightened her skirt. She'd tried to dress conservatively, but Sean had the feeling that her dinosaur earring and purple plastic shoes might give her away.

"So you don't think your dad'll eventually give in and help you?" Brooke asked, standing up and stretching.

"No way. And I won't ask him to. I'll have to apply for a loan, too. I called the training program, and they told me I can't work during the school term. I guess you're in class or rehearsal about ten hours a day." Allie looked thrilled at the thought. "So," she bolstered, "I just have to head over to the big mall. Somebody's got to need summer help. Right?"

"Right!" cheered Brooke and Sean.

Allie stepped off the curb. She lost her nerve. "Brooke, you wouldn't feel like coming with me, would you?"

Brooke unhooked the hammer from the loop in her overalls and held it up apologetically. "I have to stay here and finish the set for the senior talent show. There isn't much time left."

They all froze for a moment, a little startled at how quickly the end of high school was rushing toward them. The prom was that coming Saturday. Sean was already working on his valedictory speech and everybody was jabbering about final projects and graduation presents, grad night and caps and gowns.

"Oh, right," Allie remembered. "We rehearsed after school yesterday till almost ten. I think our skit part is going to be pretty good."

Sean slung his arm over Brooke's shoulder. "Al, Nick's dropping me downtown so I can return that tape recorder. It's due back at Payson's today. If you want I'll ask around the stores there." He and Brooke headed into campus. "Maybe I'll stop at the Bubble Café and tell them I know an artistic type who knows just where to put the pickle on the burger."

They all laughed again. "Thanks a lot." Allie bravely started for the bus stop. "Let me know if you see any signs."

" 'ALLIE WANTED.' I will. 'Bye."

"Good luck," Brooke yelled. "Call me to-night."

"Okay. 'Bye."

Sean and Brooke waved, and Allie strode across the parking lot to wait for the city bus.

She sat on the wooden bench, watching the traffic and stewing over the whole thing with her dad and the training program and the urgent necessity of finding a job. She knew why Sean was teasing her—that she could turn the simple act of finding employment into the world's most dramatic quest. She had to be practical this time, to prove to her father and herself that she could face this problem and tackle it head-on. But she didn't feel very practical. Even after all the good things that had happened to her senior year, she still had this scary feeling that if she made one wrong move, her talent, her confidence, and her acceptance to acting school could disappear. Poof. Just like it had never existed. Allie had to make sure that didn't happen.

Meanwhile, she noticed that the monster blue bus was nowhere in sight. Allie was getting impatient. The only vehicles on the street were cars spewing exhaust, a furniture truck, and a put-putting motor scooter. Soon the put-putting got louder, and there were huge circles of exhaust, so thick that it took Allie a moment to realize that a car had pulled up to the curb in front of her. It was a green Mercedes sedan, old and banged up. The engine was so noisy that the driver had to yell and hang out the window to get her attention.

"Well, hey! Allie Simon, right?"

Allie squinted through the gray smoke. She could vaguely make out a handsome young man, slightly older than she. He had a blond mustache and was wearing a tweed jacket with leather elbow patches. Allie knew she'd seen him before, but she couldn't remember where or when.

"It's Derek. Derek Jamison," he reminded her.

Allie's mind was still a blank.

"Don't you remember me?" Derek showed a hint of annoyance. "We met last week at Redwood College, outside your dad's room. I'm the poet."

"Oh, yeah." Allie resisted telling him that even Shakespeare himself wouldn't have made an impression on her that afternoon. And Derek was infinitely less interesting to her than William Shakespeare. "I remember now."

Derek turned off the engine and rested his elbows on the window frame. "Are you waiting for a ride?"

Allie nodded and checked the traffic again. No sign of the stupid bus.

"Where do you need to go? I'll take you."

"That's okay."

"No, really. I don't mind. It doesn't look like the bus is coming."

"No, thanks." Allie figured Derek wasn't a weirdo or anything, just a slightly obnoxious college boy. Still, she felt funny about getting in a car with a guy she didn't really know. "I'll wait."

Derek watched her for a moment, then finally got out and propped himself against the side of

his car. "Listen, Allie," he said in a more inti-
mate voice, "I didn't just happen to drive by
here accidentally. I've been by about four times.
Looking for you."

"Looking for me?"

He seemed to blush. "Yeah. I wanted to see if
you wanted to go out sometime. On a date."

Allie had to smile. Even though she wasn't
really interested in this guy, she was flattered.
After all, he was good-looking and in college.
"Thanks," she said more sweetly, "but I'm really
busy right now. Graduation's coming up, and
I'm rehearsing for this talent show. Plus I have
to find a summer job. . . ."

He took a step toward her and teased, "Do
you expect me to believe that you don't have
one single Friday or Saturday night free?"

Allie shrugged coyly.

"How about this Friday night?"

"I'm rehearsing."

"Okay. Next Friday."

"I'm rehearsing then, too."

"The Friday after that."

Allie started to giggle. "I think that's senior
awards night."

He moved closer, sensing that he was wearing
her down. "You're a tough one. How about this
Saturday night?"

"This Saturday night is our prom. Actually,
I'm not going, but I promised to help my friend
Brooke get ready."

His smile vanished for a second and he looked
distracted, as if he'd just remembered something. "Oh, right," he mumbled. "But you're not

73

going, though?" He smiled again. "I agree with you. Proms are dumb."

"No, they're not. I wish I was going. I'd love to go."

"You would?"

"Sure. I just don't have a date."

Derek's eyebrows came together in a funny way, as if he were figuring out a math problem or fighting a bad headache. Suddenly he patted his back pocket, making sure he had something. He sat down next to her, very close, and slid his arm over the back of the bench. When he spoke this time he sounded as if he were afraid someone would overhear. "Would you go out with me if I could take you to your senior prom?"

Allie cracked up, her classic, loud, explosive giggle. Derek looked a little uncomfortable at the amount of noise she was making, but he didn't take his eyes off her. "Come on," she sputtered. "It's a little late. They stopped selling tickets two weeks ago."

He reached to that back pocket again and pulled out a small envelope. "Well, what do you think of these?"

He wouldn't let go of the envelope while Allie peeked inside. Sure enough, there were two tickets to the Redwood High prom! "Where did you get those?" Allie shrieked. "I don't believe it."

He held a finger to her lips to shush her. "My secret. So will you go with me to your senior prom?"

Allie had one more hesitant moment, but it passed quickly. What the heck! she decided. Why shouldn't she make a big splash at the end of her high school career? She had more to celebrate than almost anyone else she knew. "Okay. Why not? Sure. I'll go."

He bit his lower lip and winked at her. The tickets disappeared and were replaced by a pen and poetry book he'd fished out of his jacket. "I guess now you'll give me your phone number and address?"

"I guess you'll need it." Allie scribbled the information on the inside cover of his book.

He read it over and smiled to himself. "I'll pick you up at eight. Maybe afterward we'll stop by my frat house for a few minutes, see if anything's going on."

"Okay."

He tucked the book back in his pocket. They both spotted the bus about half a block away, and Derek scurried back to his car, rushing to get it out of the bus stop in time. The Mercedes putputted to life again, and he swung back into traffic. "See you Saturday," he called happily.

"See *you* Saturday," Allie repeated.

Derek gunned the motor and sped away.

Allie stood up and stared at the traffic until the bus was waiting in front of her. "Well, what do you know," she giggled as she climbed up and dug in her bag for change. "See you Saturday."

"Rats!"

Sean could see as he waddled up to Payson's Stereo store that he was too late. The lights in the display window had just gone out, and the sign was being flipped from OPEN to SORRY WE MISSED YOU. Balancing the heavy tape recorder against his chest, he hurried to the door.

"Can't you let me in? I have to return this!"

He shouldn't have hung around so long at school, but Nick had insisted on watching the track workouts. Nick kept saying it was research for some new article, but Sean was sure there was more to it. But when he asked if things were okay, Nick got all moody and by the time Nick snapped out of it and convinced Sean that, no, he really didn't want to talk, if was after five. Now Payson's would probably charge him for a whole extra week.

"Hey!" Sean yelled again, trying to keep hold of the machine and free up a hand to pound the door. "Be a sport. Open up!"

He had the check from the senior class treasury in his pocket, made out for the exact amount. The additional charge would have to come out of his own money, the stash he'd been saving to spend on the prom and grad night and the great time he was going to have with Brooke. . . .

He pressed his nose into the door and tried to see inside. "Can't you open up again for two minutes!!!"

Sean suddenly found himself falling forward into thin air. The door he had been leaning against seemed to have collapsed of its own accord. It was like being Superman and walking through a wall, only Sean knew in an instant that if he hit the floor, unlike Superman, both he and the tape recorder would stumble to the ground with a shatter and a thunk.

76

"Well, look who's here! Hey, I know you. I never forget a weenie's face."

Sean stopped breathing. He didn't hit the floor, but he almost wished he had. Anything would have been better than staring into those eyes, eyes that were dark and tiny like blueberries. Eyes that brought back memories Sean never wanted to remember. It was the face that had haunted him since he was a freshman, and it hadn't gotten any less ugly in the intervening years. It was Jay Creary.

"Can't say I remember your weenie name, though," Jay said, looking Sean up and down and laughing.

Sean knew Jay was remembering plenty — when Sean was a scrawny freshman and Jay and his bully pals had taped him to the Redwood High flagpole. Jay's cackle brought it all back. The sound of electrical tape being ripped off of a brand-new roll. Jay threatening that if Sean ever tried to pay him back he'd pants Sean and tape him to the plumbing in the girls' bathroom. "I'm Sean Pendleton," Sean stated in an overly deep voice.

That struck Jay as hilarious. "Sean Pendleton," he mimicked, making fun of Sean's attempt to be macho. "So, what's your problem, Sean Pendleton?"

They were still standing in the doorway, Jay guarding the entrance. It finally occurred to Sean that Jay worked there. Sean hadn't seen him there before, and it made him even sicker to realize that Jay was a salesman at a place as enviable as Payson's. "Did you have to open the door like that?"

Sean accused, hoping to put Jay on the defensive.

"I thought you wanted in. Wasn't that why you were yelling your weenie head off?"

"I did want in."

"Well now you're in. So what?"

Sean tried to see past Jay, hoping to find someone else to help him. No such luck. "I rented a tape machine from you guys, and I want to return it. Do you mind?"

Jay finally cleared the entrance. He shifted his shoulders, and Sean noticed that he was wearing a letter jacket with a fancy letter. Jay not only had a great job at Payson's, he'd already lettered at college! The unfairness of it all made Sean want to scream. Jay nodded at the counter. "Leave it there."

Sean carefully carried it over. Jay followed, hovering, then standing threateningly close. He didn't tower over Sean as much as he had three years ago, but he still outbulked him by about fifty pounds. Sean wondered if Jay's college letter was for football, shot put, or sumo wrestling.

"I hope you didn't mess it up," Jay said, crouching down and going over the machine as if he were looking for insect eggs.

"No, I didn't mess it up," Sean came right back. "As a matter of fact, there was a broken solder joint in the V.U. meter. I soldered it back."

"Oh, so you did mess around with it."

"I said, I fixed it. . . ." Sean wanted to call Jay meathead, moron, scum — to show that he could no longer be pushed around. But he stopped himself. He was afraid to go that far.

"So how are we supposed to know if you fixed it or you broke it?"

Sean pulled out his receipt and wrote a furious note, explaining exactly what he had done. "Just show this to your repair guy. Okay?" he slapped down the senior class check and started for the door. He was eager to get out of there as if there had been a radiation leak. But suddenly a white card in the front window caught his eye and he had to stop. HELP WANTED.

"Allie," Sean whispered to himself. He turned back. "Uh, Jay?"

"What, weenie."

Sean gritted his teeth. "What kind of job is this, that you need somebody for? Does the person have to know about stereos?"

"No. We need somebody who knows how to pick lint out of their belly button." Jay laughed at his own joke. "What do you think?"

Sean found Jay's laugh physically painful. But for Allie's sake, he kept going. "I just want to know what kind of job it is, all right? I'm asking for a friend of mine."

"You have friends?" Jay howled now. "So, you think you help 'em get a job, and they'll give you a discount on your car stereo."

"Never mind." Sean cursed under his breath. He had to get out of here. Jay was even worse than he remembered. This probably wasn't a job that Allie would be suited for anyway. And besides, if he stayed here getting taunted by Jay, who knows what he'd do. This was like reliving a nightmare.

"Hey, I think it's really you that's interested in the job." Jay decided suddenly. He got a sugary smile on his face and his eyes twinkled like grimy tin. "But I have to tell you, we don't hire weenies in this store."

"Forget I asked," Sean exhaled. He turned around and stomped out, hitting his fist against a concrete wall.

"ARRRRRRRHHHHHHHH!"

Sean bit back tears. He kept thinking back to freshman year, and the fact that he was going to be a freshman again. If he had to live through that whole cycle another time, he might not survive it. Maybe the world was going to be filled with Jay Crearys. All with great jobs and college letters. All waiting for the Sean Pendletons to bully and humiliate. Sean hoped that it wouldn't be that way. He prayed that it wouldn't. But when he took one last look at Payson's front door, he had an awful feeling that his prayers were not going to be answered.

CHAPTER 8

Coffee beans. Rich, round coffee beans. The smell was almost overpowering, and it made Derek feel slightly dizzy. Still, he breathed in deeply, because at least the smell was pleasant. Better than the taste. Maybe if he drank coffee half filled with milk or chocolate Haagen Dazs, it would be okay. But straight, black and bitter, even with the cinnamon they brewed into it at the Underground college café — it made his mouth pucker and his stomach ache. But everybody else seemed to love it, just like that awful beer his frat brothers chugged and the weedy pipe his poetry professor smoked. So Derek had decided he'd learn to love it, too.

"Want your coffee warmed up?" Celia asked, suddenly looming over him with a full pot in her hand.

Instinctively Derek's hand covered the top of his cup. He buried his nose in his notebook and pretended that he was too absorbed to look up. The steam from her coffee pot made him break out in a sweat. "Let me finish this, babe."

"Derek, I'm off work in a few minutes. If you want something to eat, you'd better tell me now."

"Uh-huh." Derek clutched his forehead, as if he were deep in calm concentration. In reality, his mind was racing, and it wasn't from the coffee. Soon he had to face her, to tell her his news. He'd put it off as long as he could. It was Friday night, for God's sake. The prom was tomorrow. If he waited much longer he might as well just stand her up without a word.

"Derek?" Celia was still waiting by the table.

"I don't want anything," he finally told her. "Thanks."

"Okay. I'll be back as soon as my last table pays their check." She gave his hair a fluff and skipped off.

Oh, man, this was confusing! Derek churned. Just like his entire freshman year at college was confusing. High school had been so much simpler. Derek had gone through Cotter Valley High with the same forty kids he'd known since kindergarten. He was popular with the girls, played soccer, worked on the yearbook, was famous for having a Mercedes — even if it was a falling apart 1971 model that he'd traded for his electric guitar and Fender amp. Everybody knew who he was in Cotter Valley. He didn't have to prove anything or make some statement to make people notice him.

But from the first week of college he wasn't sure how to fit in. Redwood didn't have a soccer

82

team. They didn't encourage freshmen on the yearbook staff, and he hadn't even made the first cut for jazz band. So he'd decided on poetry, with the fraternity as backup. And, so far, it had worked out pretty well. He'd survived rush. His poetry prof wrote encouraging comments on his papers. And Celia had fallen for him.

That was the real problem. He'd pursued Celia because she was gorgeous and all the frat guys noticed her when they hung out at the Underground to drink coffee. But Derek didn't really like Celia all that much. She was too nervous, too unsure of who she was, a quality that didn't make him feel any more at ease. And besides, she was still in high school! His frat brothers didn't know that and he'd never hear the end of it if they did — they thought that any guy who still dated high school girls just didn't have the stuff to attract a sorority sister.

Of course, Allie Simon was still in high school, too, but there was something about her that really got to Derek. She had a sense of style, of knowing who she was. Maybe she wasn't beautiful like Celia, but she was offbeat, an actress, the right kind of girl friend for a struggling poet. Besides, something about her wild laugh and big waif eyes made him go weak in the knees.

"How am I going to do this?" he groaned to himself.

But before he could think of an answer, Celia was back. She flopped into the chair across from him and dumped two fistfuls of change onto the table. She built little stacks. Quarters. Dimes. Nickels and pennies. "I did pretty well tonight," she smiled, looking at her tips. After she counted each stack, she playfully dropped it in her apron pocket.

Why did she have to look so dewy and satisfied all of a sudden? Why couldn't she be at her most insecure and uptight? That would have made what Derek was about to do so much easier. There was a crash as somebody dropped a tray of dishes in the kitchen. One table applauded and Celia looked up, tossing her lovely yellow hair and giggling.

Derek took out his pipe and nervously chomped on the mouthpiece.

"So what's up?" she asked cheerily, finished with her money counting. "I thought you had to study tonight. I didn't think I'd see you until tomorrow."

He nodded and cleared his throat.

"Wait until you see my prom dress," she flirted. "Oh — lots of couples are wearing one thing the same — like a matching ribbon and handkerchief or something. Do you want to do that? Or do you think it's too dumb? I could run out tomorrow morning and find something — if you think it's okay."

"Actually, Celia, that's what I wanted to talk to you about. Why I came by tonight."

She lit up. "About finding something that matches? You'd really do that?"

"Well, no. Not exactly that. No."

"What then?"

"Well, about your prom. . . ."

"Yes?"

She looked so sunny, so giddy and expectant,

that he didn't know if he could do it . . . but he had to. Forcing himself to get it over with, he pushed away his coffee cup and blurted, "I know it's kind of late to tell you this, but, I just found out that I have to go, um, to San Francisco tomorrow night for this poetry reading. It's very important — these people asked me to come and read my poem myself, and I couldn't turn them down. I just couldn't." He finally looked up. "I knew you'd understand."

She stared at him as if he were speaking a foreign language. "What?"

"Tomorrow night. I know I said we'd go to your prom and all, but this came up and it was too important to say no."

Her face had gone whiter than the little pitcher of cream on the center of the table. It took a moment for her to speak again. "Are you telling me that you're backing out of taking me to my senior prom?"

"Well, uh . . . yes. Yes, I am. I have to."

"Derek, it's tomorrow night!"

"I know. I know. And believe me, I would have given you more notice if I could, but this just came up, um, just today, and I thought it over and I knew you'd decide that this was more important than some dumb prom." He tried to laugh. His voice came out like a stale cracker.

"I don't believe this," Celia stuttered, almost to herself. "I don't believe you'd tell me this the night before the prom. Do you know how long I saved to buy that dress? How much this means to me?"

His stomach was really starting to ache now.

"I understand how you could be angry at me." He quickly pulled a flyer and two movie passes out of his notebook. "That's why I got these for you. Passes for that French movie on campus tomorrow night." He pushed the paper toward her. "Like I told you before, it's a lot more interesting than some silly prom." She wouldn't touch the passes. "See, I even got you two. I figured you might be mad at me, so you can even take some other guy. I don't mind."

"I can't believe this is happening," she repeated, staring in front of her. Derek knew that she didn't want to look at him because she was afraid she'd start crying. "What am I supposed to do now?"

"I'm sorry."

"You're sorry? That's all you have to say? You're sorry!" Her tears started to gush, and Derek glanced around, hoping that none of his frat brothers were witnessing this. "Look," she stammered, "why don't you just give me the prom tickets. Maybe I can get somebody else to go with me. God knows who — the night before — but maybe I can find someone."

Derek pushed the movie passes toward her. He had to move ahead with his plan. There was no way he was going to let her show up at the prom and discover him there with another girl. "I don't have the prom tickets anymore. I, uh, tore them up."

"You WHAT!" Now there was rage behind the tears.

"I didn't think you'd want them." Derek decided to go on the attack. He wasn't sure how

86

else to handle this. "I told you, proms are stupid. If you want to do something worthwhile, go to that movie on campus. What else do you except from me?"

She stood up and crumpled the movie passes in her fist. "I expected more from you than this," she said in much too loud a voice. "You really are low, Derek."

"Oh, Celia. Come on."

"You sleaze."

"Now, now."

"You are . . . a . . . a . . ." — she searched for the words — "phony, insensitive, overbearing creep."

"Celia!"

"And you know what else?"

"What?" he asked faintly.

"YOUR POETRY SUCKS!"

Derek tried to maintain his composure as she threw the passes in his face, knocking over her chair, and stormed out of the Underground Café.

Celia walked up her street as though she were staggering home from the wars. The ride on the bus had taken a lot of the anger out of her. Now there was a kind of dull grief and shock — shock over not going to the prom, shock over the way Derek had told her. Her arms were heavy, her face puffy from all the tears, the inside of her head felt like a matted cotton ball.

One of the porch lights was burned out over her front door, and Celia was glad. It made it too dark to see the blistered paint and the battered lawn chairs. She climbed up the steps, almost stumbling. She was relieved to notice that her mother's car wasn't in the driveway and remembered that her mom had a date. Good. The last thing she needed right now was having to explain her red eyes and swollen face.

"He would have dumped me sooner or later," she mumbled, pausing on the Astroturf. It probably started that day her mother stopped by the café. Come to think of it, that *was* about when Derek began to lose interest. She could hear his frat brothers ragging him — asking which one Derek was dating, the young one or her mother. Hee, hee, hee. That was probably when Derek decided that no sorority would give her two looks, and that she wasn't really worth his time, either.

Celia didn't want to think about it anymore. She was tired of crying, tired of hurting, tired of trying to figure out what to do with a formal dress she couldn't afford and a head full of dreams that had suddenly turned to dust. She dug in her purse for her keys. But before she unlocked the door, it swung open.

"Hi," said Nick, looking sleepy and sad.

Celia wasn't surprised to see him. He'd slept in their living room almost every other night for the last week. She pushed past him without a word and headed for her room. Nick watched her. Once inside, she slammed her bedroom door. She threw down her purse and her waitress apron, sending quarters and nickels rolling across the floor.

There was a knock. "You okay?" Nick called.

Celia didn't want to answer. She felt the tears

pressing again and, a second later, her cheeks were soaking.

Nick knocked once more. Softly. "Cici?"

Celia stood very still for a moment, as if she could will herself to vanish into air. Then the door opened, and Nick was standing there.

"Hi?" he inquired, his voice full of concern.

Celia wept.

"Come on," he comforted, putting his arm around her and leading her back out into the living room. She sobbed while he cleared his sweat shirt, some notebooks, and a pair of dumbbells off the couch. He sat her down.

"That creep," Celia wailed.

"What creep?"

"That selfish jerk!"

"Who?"

"That mean, inconsiderate piece of slime."

"Cici, who are you talking about?"

"Derek. Derek Jamison! He turned out to be a total slimeball."

"Ah. Well, I could have told you that." Celia glared and Nick shrugged. He'd met Derek once, picking Celia up at the café. Nick had not been impressed. He patted Celia's shoulder. "Sorry. I couldn't resist."

"You were right." She burst into tears again.

"What happened? Did you break up with him?"

"You could say that." She shook her head as if she still couldn't believe it. Her voice came out in fits and starts. "He ditched out of the prom. He waited until tonight to tell me. He didn't even give me the tickets so I could try and get somebody else. Although, God knows who I could get at the last minute like this."

"He backed out on you tonight?" Nick was as full of disbelief as she. "He is a slimebag."

Celia nodded. "This is the worst day of my life."

Nick fetched her a box of Kleenex and sat with her while she blew her nose and blotted her eyes. Her crying finally stopped and she stared dully out the window. The wind rustled the trees, and somewhere down the block a dog whimpered.

"You know what we could do," Nick said after a long time.

"What."

He shifted. "I don't know. It might be too weird for you."

"Nick, what?"

"Well, you might think this is a bad idea — but I bought prom tickets, because of that dumb king nomination, and then I never asked anybody because . . . well, just because. Anyway, I could borrow my brother's tux. If you want, we could go together. You and me."

Celia's puffy eyes opened wide. It took her a moment to digest Nick's invitation. Most girls would have been on cloud nine, going to the prom with Nicholas Rhodes. But she was Nick's cousin. Showing up with him would be like advertising to the entire class that she couldn't get a real date. Of course, if she didn't go with Nick, her dress would hang unused in her closet, and for the rest of her life, she'd wonder what it would have been like to attend her one and only senior prom. "Wouldn't you feel strange? People might think it's pathetic that you had to go with your cousin."

"I don't *have* to go with you," Nick came back right away. "I *want* to go with you."

Celia smiled. She knew that Nick was trying to make her feel better, but that also, unlike her, he really didn't care what people thought. "Are you sure?"

"Why not?"

"Who knows? Maybe we'd even have fun."

"Sure. At least I won't have to worry about making a good impression. I can step on your toes, tell dumb jokes, drip gravy on my tux. It'll be great."

Celia's grief was starting to drift away. "I guess neither of us will have to be on good behavior. We can be our dopey, normal selves."

"Sounds good to me." Nick looked around the living room. "I'd tell you what time I was picking you up, but since I'll probably be in the next room, maybe you should come get me."

He was trying to make a joke, but she saw that sadness reappear on his face. "You're not going home?"

He looked away. "Maybe just to get some stuff. I'm starting to like it here."

Both of them laughed.

"Okay, Nick. Let's go together. It's a deal."

"Great."

Celia stood up. Her whole body felt tired. "I'd better go to sleep. This has been kind of a long day."

"I bet." Nick picked up his notebook and settled back onto on the couch.

Celia turned back. "Thanks, Nick. I really needed a friend."

"We all do."

They smiled at each other and she padded off to her room.

CHAPTER 9

"It's senior maadnesssssss!"

"The Class of '88 is great!!"

"Ready or not, world, we are coming!"

"WAAAAAAH HOOOOOOOOOO!!!"

The Redwood High prom was as glittery as every senior dreamed it would be. Every inch of the Palace Hotel ballroom was white, sparkling, lit up, and grand. Silver helium balloons floated about like drunken planets. Curly confetti dangled down from the chandeliers. The music platform was trimmed in tinsel and the band members' jackets were gold lamé.

Meg was in the midst of it all — on the dance floor. Loud voices and music surrounding her. Everywhere she looked she saw glistening satin, rented tuxes, swaying hips, and fast feet. Patrick was wilting, but she couldn't sit down. She wanted that rush again, the constant motion and music and sparkling chaos in the center of the floor.

"I think Joanne's supposed to announce the king and queen soon," Patrick called to her. They were so packed in that if she danced in another direction she lost him completely.

"WHAT?"

"ANNOUNCE SOON." Patrick wriggled closer. He moved as if his powder-blue tux was too stiff and his polished shoes too tight. "KING AND QUEEN."

"SOMETHING'S GREEN?"

"WHAT?"

"Patrick, I can't hear . . . NEVER MIND." She laughed and fell forward. Patrick reached out to catch her.

The drummer reeled into a wild solo, and they all stopped dancing to watch. He slammed and clanged like a wind-up toy, flailing his way to a rousing finish. The seniors clapped, and the lead singer made a fierce pumping motion with his arm.

"All right. Class of '88!" the singer rasped after the music stopped. The band took a bow, and the singer approached the mike again. "Folks, I'd like to introduce your president, Joanne Fantozzi. She has some announcements to make. Then we're going to play another set, and after that, we'll let you rest and have some chow." There was more applause and a little roaming around as the lights came up, and Joanne climbed to the stage. She was wearing a ruffly white dress and holding two small envelopes.

"Good luck, Meg," Patrick whispered.

They waited while the singer readjusted the

mike stand for Joanne. Meg took that moment to look around the ballroom. She'd run into Brooke and Sean on the dance floor, stomping happily and having a great time. Brooke had yelled something about Allie getting asked at the last minute and being in back with the drama kids. Meg craned her neck to look for her. But she only saw Nick and Celia at a sideline table. Celia seemed to be holding up. And Nick . . . well, he seemed relaxed and jolly in that typical Nick way. Meg quickly looked away.

"Is everybody having fun?" Joanne was yelling into the mike. Her voice was painfully loud.

"YEEEEEEEEESSSSSSSSSSS!!!!!!!!!"

Joanne giggled. She looked to Miss Meyer, the class adviser who stood at the edge of the stage, holding two crowns made out of cardboard, tin foil, and plastic jewels. When Miss Meyer gave a nod, Joanne leaned into the microphone again. "It's time to announce the winners for prom king and queen. I have to say, though, it was pretty stiff competition and I think all eight people nominated are already winners. Actually, I'd say that this is an entire senior class of winners!"

There was another roar that only ended when Joanne started to tear open the first envelope. By the time she pulled out the card the room had become very, very quiet. "The prom queen for the Redwood High Class of '88 is. . . ." She stopped to look at the name and smiled. "Someone who has worked hard for our class since we were freshmen. Over the years she's been our class president, treasurer, vice-president, and this year she's on the senior events committee, while also making honor roll and lettering in track. Let's hear it for . . . MEG McCALL!"

Patrick hugged Meg as the crowd cheered. But as delighted as Meg was to win, she felt strangely disconnected, as if she were watching herself on film.

"Meg, go on up to the stage," Patrick prodded.

"Oh. Okay."

The seniors made an aisle for her. As she passed by, they patted and congratulated. Joanne gestured for Meg to say a few words at the mike.

"Um, thanks everybody. Thanks a lot," was all Meg could think of to say. She was suddenly on the verge of tears. Everyone laughed when she had to crouch down so tiny Miss Meyer could place the crown on her head. When Meg stood up, she saw Patrick gazing at her with terrific pride and adoration.

Joanne stepped up to the mike again. "The prom king for the Class of '88 is. . . ." She paused to open the envelope and Meg looked to Patrick. He took a few steps closer, ready to stride up to the stage and stand next to her. "Someone who has lettered in football, basketball, and track, and is one of the best reporters on *The Guardian* and an all-around great guy . . . NICHOLAS RHODES!"

Meg's eyes opened wide. Just hearing Nick's name jolted her. She watched him run to the stage. He was wearing a black tux and hightopped tennis shoes. Smiling broadly, he took the crown from Miss Meyer, set it on his head himself, and stepped up to the mike.

96

Seniors whistled and stomped. Nick finally held up a hand to quiet them. "We were the first freshman class at Redwood High, the first class to be here all four years, and I'd say we'll go down in history as one of the best classes ever." Nick's crown slipped off and everyone laughed as he caught it and plopped it back on his head. "Thanks! This is great!"

Nick was already off the stage and horsing around with some of his newspaper buddies when Joanne took the mike one last time and announced, "Now our prom king and queen will start off the next dance. So everybody clear some space and give them room!"

Meg froze. She was supposed to dance with Nick! In front of everyone! The disconnected feeling had turned to trembly panic. She wanted to run to Patrick, to back off the floor like all the other seniors, or crawl under the tinsel and the tablecloths. But Nick was walking toward her, his familiar green eyes fixed on hers.

The song was slow and sultry. A saxophone wailed. The voices sang in sweet harmony. Nick politely held out his hand, but Meg didn't take it. Instead she walked past him, leading the way to the middle of the floor. He followed.

Meg couldn't look at Nick as they awkwardly arranged themselves in a formal dance position, his hand on her waist, her hand on his shoulder, their palms barely touching. Slowly, they began to dance. Meg felt every eye in the room on her. She smiled at Patrick, at Celia, at Joanne, and at Miss Meyer. She kept herself at arm's distance. But the more she tried not to be aware of Nick,

97

the more powerfully she felt his hand and his arm and his shoulder brushing her cheek.

Suddenly there was a ripple of laughter in the crowd and Meg realized that her crown was toppling forward. She tried to grab it, and then Nick tried to help her, which only made his crown tumble off, too. A second later everybody was giggling and applauding as Meg and Nick fell to their knees to pick up their homemade crowns.

"How low the mighty have fallen!" kidded Sam Pond.

"That was a quick reign," Sean laughed.

"Who made those crowns?" objected Maria Martinez.

Everybody continued to laugh and tease, but Meg heard only one voice.

"Meg," Nick whispered while they were kneeling and their faces were very close.

Their eyes locked. Everything else faded away.

Nick touched her hand. "Remember me?"

Meg had to close her eyes. She was reeling.

He reached past her, as if he'd been reaching for the crowns the whole time and touching her had been an accident. He tossed the crowns to Joanne, then helped Meg up. They stared at each other.

"Okay!" yelled Joanne, her hands cupped around her mouth. "Let's all join them. This dance is dedicated to the future of the Class of '88!"

As couples filled in around them, Nick and Meg came together again. But instead of taking a formal dance position this time, Nick reached

98

both hands around her waist. Briefly Meg resisted. What would Patrick think if he saw them dancing like that? But the dance floor was dense as a forest. Before she could think any more, her arms had encircled Nick's neck.

He pulled her closer.

They barely moved. The couples around them dipped and swayed, but Meg stood motionless. Nick's cheek against hers. Shallow breathing. Warm skin. Silky hair. Then he looked into her eyes and her face turned up. Closer. Their lips brushed. Just barely. It was all so slow and blurry and breathless that Meg wasn't sure what was happening. Suddenly the music stopped and Meg backed away. Fast now. Terrified. She turned, rushing off, searching for Patrick. Patrick! But Nick caught her hand and pulled her to him.

"Meet me outside in about ten minutes," he said in an urgent whisper. "By the swimming pool."

Meg no longer felt as if she were outside herself. Now her insides were a live wire. "I can't."

"Nobody will see us. I have to talk to you."

The band launched into a fast rock song. Meg knocked into Deb Dryden and almost stumbled over Tom Albrecht.

Nick called to her one more time. "Meg, it's important."

Meg didn't allow herself to hear another word. She pushed her way back through the dancers until she stood safely next to unsuspecting Patrick.

But ten minutes later she was outside, waiting

just inside the chain link fence that surrounded the pool. She could barely hear the band anymore. Light flickered from TV sets in the hotel rooms above. Water lapped concrete. A cold breeze blew and she hugged her bare arms.

There was a rustle, then soft footsteps. "Meg," she heard Nick whisper.

It took her a moment to find him. He was only a few yards away, but the plants were so lush and the shadows so thick that she could barely see.

"Meg, you decided to come."

She joined Nick at the fence, keeping a safe distance. They both stood very still. "I can't stay."

"I know."

"I told Patrick I was going to look for Allie."

A sudden gust of wind blew Meg's hair across her cheek and mouth. Nick's hand rose gently, as if he were going to smooth the strands away. But he reconsidered and, instead, tightly clasped his palms in front of him.

"Nick, what did you need to tell me?" Meg tried to sound friendly but cool.

He cleared his throat and looked around, making sure no one else was near. "All right." He stared at the ground. "I have to tell you this because . . . I guess we're graduating, and we probably won't see each other much at college. And because I feel like if I keep anything more inside me I might just go crazy." He paused, then began again. "Maybe it's selfish of me, but I just want to tell you, and then I won't bother you anymore."

He stopped. Meg was trying hard to keep her face expressionless and her hands still. Her insides were going haywire.

100

"I love you," Nick said suddenly. He didn't wait for her to respond, but rambled, "I think I always have. I don't know when I figured it out. Maybe last year, maybe a long time before that." He stepped back. "I know that you're with Patrick, and I don't want to do anything to get in the way of that. I guess I don't know what I want. Maybe just to be friends again and forget all the weird stuff that's happened between us over the years and even what's happening right now. I guess that's it. I just want to be friends again." He gave a sad, embarrassed sigh and shook his head. "I shouldn't have done this to you. I'm sorry. Things have been so crazy for me lately."

Another cold breeze blew. Meg didn't feel it. Nick extended his hand to shake. "Friends?"

She stared at his open palm. She was a radio stuck on a single station, receiving only his hand, his voice, his eyes, his golden hair, and sad smile.

Nick shifted nervously when she didn't take his hand. "Is it okay . . . to be friends . . . after what I told you?"

Meg tried to make her mouth move. She turned away and looked back toward the pool and the fence and the banquet rooms. There was the crunch of someone collecting ice with a metal scoop and the wind rustling the trees.

"Meg."

She was paralyzed. Stuck.

"Meg, please."

"What?"

"Say something!"

"I . . . I don't know what to say."

"Are you mad at me?"

"No."

"I'm sorry. I shouldn't have told you, I. . . ."

"Oh, Nick."

"Yes?"

She couldn't talk anymore, or think — no planning now, no reason or doubt. She just threw herself against him, and his arms engulfed her. Warm, strong Nick, the same arms that had pulled her up into the tree house a million times when they were kids. The arms that had tickled her, teased her, hugged her when she hurt.

"I love you, too," she breathed.

Then they were kissing, wildly, knowing this might be the only time they'd ever be together like this. Nick kissing her hair, her forehead, her cheeks, her mouth, her neck. She kissing him back just as fiercely and clinging to him as if someone were about to pry them apart.

"I love you, Nick," she heard herself say, louder this time. "I have forever."

Then there was a clank of the metal gate swinging open. Meg pulled back, pushing Nick away with the flat of her hand. She was terrified now. Shaking. They both froze to see who was passing by, but it was only a hotel guest, humming to himself and carrying a bucket of ice. After the man trotted up to his room, Nick took her in his arms again.

"I have to get back." She panicked, struggling free.

"Not yet."

"Patrick's waiting for me."

"Just a few more minutes — "

"I can't! Patrick — "

102

"I know all about Patrick!" Nick flared suddenly.

Meg put her face in her hands. Now she felt so confused she thought she'd go crazy. "I have to go back inside," she said after a moment.

Nick slowly touched her cheek. He rested his forehead on her shoulder. "In a minute."

Her hand floated up to caresss his hair. "Why now?" she said, almost to herself. She began to cry, very softly. "Why do we have to figure this out now? It'll never work."

He kissed her neck. "I know."

"It never has."

His arms crept up her back.

"Patrick, he's...."

"Waiting."

"I have to go."

"Yes."

She kissed him. "I'm leaving now."

"Okay."

"Good-bye."

"Good-bye, Meg."

Neither of them took a step.

Back inside the ballroom, Celia was very glad she hadn't stayed home. It was a good idea after all, she'd realized, showing up with Nick. She knew she looked terrific — everybody had told her so — and so far, there had been no snide comments or insinuating looks about why her date happened to also be a close relative. Maybe it wasn't the most romantic evening of her life, but it was a night she'd always remember.

Since Nick had gone out — to talk with the

guys, he'd said — three boys had asked Celia to
dance. She'd finally accepted Howard Swain, and
even though Nancy Carlin, Howard's date, looked
a little miffed, Celia wanted to show herself off
on the dance floor. It was a hot song, and Joanne
had started this goofy line dance, where people
were holding on to the person in front of them and
doing silly steps and kicks. It was kind of like the
old bunny hop, and everybody was laughing their
heads off and having a great time.

Howard joined the line and Celia jumped in
after him. They hopped and wiggled around the
entire dance floor, snaking back and forth, ducking under each other's arms and splitting off to
form new lines. Giddy from the motion and the
music, Celia let go of Howard's waist and led a
line on her own, about twenty kids following behind her. She headed into the last unexplored
corner of the ballroom, weaving her way around
tables and chairs, her line growing longer and
longer as she leaped and kicked.

She threw her head back. She laughed. She
kicked higher and higher. She was in the middle
of a split-leg stag leap over a heap of fallen confetti when she saw something that stunned her.
Her legs went stiff and her stomach turned to
stone. She stopped so suddenly that everyone behind slammed into one another like dominos.
They all recovered instantly, giggling and grop-
ing, but Celia pried herself free. The stone turned
to molten lava, and she wondered if she'd suddenly been overcome with exhaustion or heat-
stroke or some rare jungle fever. Any explanation
had to make more sense that what she was seeing.

What was Derek Jamison doing at her senior prom?!

He was wearing a white jacket and bow tie and lecturing to a group of drama kids. Celia's line hopped on without her, and she scrambled farther away to watch him, but hopefully, not let him see her. He didn't. He was too busy trying to impress the girl he was with, some drama girl in a kimono and satin bloomers. The girl had an enormous ribbon around her streaked hair as if she were a Christmas parcel, and something about her was very, very familiar. Then the girl jerked back to remove Derek's arm from her shoulder, and Celia saw the whole picture.

It was Allie. Her ex-best friend. Derek had dumped her so he could take Allie instead! Celia Cavenaugh was a complete and total fool.

Praying no one would see her, Celia strode furiously toward the exit. She had to find somewhere — a bathroom, a phone booth, a closet, *anywhere* — where she could be alone. She blindly made her way out of the ballroom and hurried down a hallway, past an elevator, into the lobby. Scuttling between bellhops and carts of luggage she searched for a hideout. She started for the front door, but just as she did, she saw Maggie Tressmen, probably the biggest mouth in the entire senior class, slip out to have a cigarette. Celia headed for the ladies' room, but then she saw Brooke Applebaum come into the lobby and head for it, too. Just then Brooke turned, as if she had some special antenna, and looked right at Celia.

Celia bolted. She saw a dark door, covered

with plump, quilted leather. She headed for it and pushed it open, entering a strange, adult place. Dark. Air-conditioner cold. The tinkle of glasses and a loose piano. There was a circle of U-shaped booths, lit only by single candles. Many of them were empty.

Celia knew it was the bar, and that she was not allowed to even sit in there, but where else could she go? Maybe she could order a soda and the waitress would let her stay. Celia slid into the first booth and listened to muffled voices and that corny piano. No waitress came. No one noticed her. Thank God. She was safe.

Finally she cradled her face in her hand and released one throaty sob. The tears followed, gushing like rapids.

"Allie," she cried. "He dumped me for Allie!"

She'd remember her senior prom, all right. She'd remember it forever. No matter how hard she would try to forget.

CHAPTER 10

"Hey, Sean," Patrick called over the laughter, "has anybody here seen Meg?"

Sean was at his table, goofing around with Greg Kendall and Sam Pond. The band had just left for their break and waiters were criss-crossing the floor, placing tiny cups of fruit salad at each dinner place. Sam juggled three strawberries while Greg picked off maraschino cherries and devoured them. "Haven't seen her since that crowning thing," Sean answered. He plucked one of Sam's strawberries out of the air and tossed it to Patrick. "Pond, I can't believe they're letting you out."

Sam grinned. "It is kind of amazing, isn't it?"

"Poor world," Greg teased.

"Look who's talking," Sam came back.

Patrick tried to get their attention again. "So you guys haven't seen her?"

107

"Oh, wait," Sam remembered. "I think I saw her go out. Yeah, sort of toward the pool."

"Thanks." Patrick started to go.

Greg called after him. "Maybe she went skinny-dipping."

"Maybe we should all go," hollered Sam. "Or at least watch!"

Patrick laughed and waved. Heading for the door, he wondered why Meg had gone outside. She said she was looking for Allie, but he'd found Allie in the corner of the ballroom with her drama friends and some obnoxious college guy date. Of course, the ballroom was as stuffy as the Redwood gym after all that dancing, so maybe Meg just went out to stick her feet in the water or — who knows — maybe she did go for a quick dip. Sometimes she did nutty things like that. Patrick smiled, thinking about how Meg would swing into the river from the highest rope, yelling like Tarzan, or climb Pilot Rock to the very top — things that he'd never attempt in a million years.

He strolled through the lobby and around the outside of the hotel, past the parking lot and the churning ice machine to where he could see the glimmer of the moon off the surface of the swimming pool. He made a move for the chain link fence but noticed a couple in the shadows. Stifling a laugh, he waited, hoping they would notice him, too, and break things up.

The pair was almost hidden by a droopy tree but he could see that they were making out like there was no tomorrow. Even from where he was standing he could tell that it was so passionate, it embarrassed him to watch. Still, he took one

108

more glance, hoping to recognize the guy. An escapade like this deserved a little ribbing at least.

But it was the girl he recognized first. The more he stared the more he saw the outline of Meg's tall, leggy frame. The moonlight was just bright enough to see the satiny blue of her dress and her silky long hair. It was Meg all right. There was no mistaking it. And Nick. Her childhood pal, Nick Rhodes, that she had stopped hanging around with about the time that she had started dating him.

Patrick backed up into the darkness again. He couldn't absorb it, couldn't even think about it. It wasn't happening, he told himself. It hadn't happened. It would never happen again. Ignore it and it would disappear.

He backed up even farther and called, "MEG. MEG, ARE YOU OUT HERE? IT'S ME. PATRICK."

He waited. There were whispers and rustles. Then she appeared, slightly winded, out of the shadows. Alone. Patrick tried to look unknowing even though his heart felt like a wrecked train. Meg could barely look at him. Her cheeks were flushed, her eyes damp, her hair wild.

"Hi," she said first. Even her voice sounded wrong.

"I just wanted to tell you that I found Allie." Patrick knew that his voice sounded off, too. "And dinner's being served. That's all."

"Oh. Thanks," she said as she scurried past him, back toward the ballroom. "I was just coming back in. I was, um, getting some air."

"I understand." Patrick stayed long enough to

spot Nick hiding by the fence. Then he followed
Meg back inside.

"Let's go back to the ballroom, Laura. I'm
telling you, they'll know right away that we're
not twenty-one."

"Jessica, come on. Let's order scotch and
grapefruit juice."

"Eww."

"All right, maybe we should have a vodka
collins. They say vodka doesn't taste so bad. And
you can't smell it on your breath, so the guys
won't be able to tell."

"Why don't we just forget it."

"Jessica, don't be such a wimp."

"I'm not a wimp. Don't call me a wimp."

Celia slid down in the padded booth as the two
seniors crept up to the bar. Laura Larson was in
Whitney Hain's snobby rich crowd, and Jessica
Westerheim was a popular gossip who'd been
nominated for prom queen. Of all the people at
the prom, Jessica and Laura were the two Celia
least wanted to see right now. Luckily though,
they were so busy trying to look old enough to
order a drink that they didn't notice Celia.

"The bartender's ignoring us," Jessica insisted.

"Just keep standing here. He'll come over."

"Okay." They waited impatiently. Finally Jessica leaned closer to Laura and said in a giggly
voice, "Did you see Celia Cavenaugh run out of
the ballroom in the middle of the line dance?"

Celia held her breath.

"No! What happened?"

"I think she freaked out or something. Maybe

because she didn't get nominated prom queen."

"Probably."

"Or maybe because she had to come as Nick's date. God, it's like going to the prom with your father or something."

They tee-heed like crazy. Celia sunk lower, drowning in humiliation.

Then a third voice cut in. It was straight-forward and a little angry. "Since when is your father the Redwood High prom king, Laura?"

Celia had to glance up. Both Jessica and Laura had stepped away from the bar with their hands on their hips to face the new girl, who was none other than Brooke Applebaum. Brooke's lacy dress was awkward, but everything else about her was graceful and sure.

"Huh?" mumbled Laura.

"Prom king," repeated Brooke. "I just meant, how could anyone be upset over going to the prom with the prom king? I'd be pretty thrilled, even if he was my cousin."

"I guess," Laura pouted.

"And as far as not being nominated queen, I didn't hear your name, Jessica, when they announced the winner."

Jessica glared. "Come on, Laura," she said, taking Laura's arm and pulling her away from the bar. "Let's get out of here. Only nerds sneak into a bar during their senior prom."

Laura gave Brooke her most condescending look. "That's right. Let's go."

With twin pert head tosses, they turned and marched out the door.

Brooke looked down the row of booths, spotting Celia right away. She walked up to the edge of the table and said softly, "Are you okay? I don't want to bother you or anything. I just saw you rush in here. You looked pretty upset."

Celia couldn't meet the warmth and concern in Brooke's brown eyes. All she could think about was junior year when she'd snubbed Brooke and told Sean not to date her because Brooke was an oddball. Now Brooke was Allie's best friend. Sometimes Celia saw Brooke, Sean, and Allie together and was more jealous of their friendship than she'd ever been of rich girls like Laura and Whitney Hain.

"I'm fine."

Brooke hesitated. "You don't look fine."

Celia twisted a cocktail napkin, drummed her fingernails on the table, played with the melted candle wax. The whole time Brooke stared at her, unmoving. Finally Celia couldn't hold it in anymore and tears rolled. Brooke slid in next to her.

"How am I supposed to go back in there?" Celia sniffled. Brooke handed her a stack of napkins from the next booth. "It's too awful. How could she do this to me? How could Allie do this to me?"

Up to this time Brooke seemed only interested in comforting Celia, not the cause of her distress. Hearing Allie's name peaked her curiosity. "What about Allie?"

"She knew I was going out with him," Celia ranted. "She had to know. She probably stole Derek away just to get me back."

"Get you back for what?"

Celia briefly glanced up at Brooke's freckled face. "You know. For last year and stuff with you. For freshman year, too. I just never thought she'd do something like this."

"Like what?"

"Make Derek dump me for the prom at the last minute. That is so low. So low!"

Brooke's eyes had grown huge. "Celia, what are you saying about Derek?"

"Don't tell me that you don't know he was supposed to take me to the prom and then yesterday he backed out so he could show up with Allie instead."

"Derek was supposed to take you? Derek Jamison!"

"Of course, Derek Jamison. Who else? Allie must really hate me to do this."

Brooke held Celia's arm. "Celia, Allie doesn't hate you, and I'm positive that she never knew anything about you and Derek."

"Oh, sure," Celia scoffed.

"Celia, Allie doesn't even like him that much. She only agreed to go because she wanted to be here tonight. She cares about you. She's told me a million times how close you guys used to be. She would never have hurt you like this if she'd known what she was doing."

Celia looked up, not sure whether to believe Brooke or not. "Really?"

"I swear."

"Allie didn't know?"

"No."

"You're sure?"

"Very."

Celia pressed a napkin to her face. Her tears had stopped. "Oh."

They sat there quietly listening to the piano plunk and the glasses clink. Finally Brooke started to get up.

Celia stopped her. "Uh, thanks for standing up for me with Jessica and Laura. Now they'll probably go around saying awful things about you."

"They have for years. I don't care."

Celia looked at her with admiration. "You really don't do you?" They both slid out of the booth and looked around. Still, no one noticed them. "I guess it's a good thing they have such bad service in here." Brooke laughed. "Tell Allie I know it's not her fault. Okay?"

"Okay."

Slowly they went back out the padded door and into the lobby. It was much brighter and busier.

"I don't think I can go back to the prom, though," Celia said, stopping at the check-in counter. "I can't face seeing Derek again. And I don't want him to see me. Do you think Nick would be okay if I left now and walked home?"

"I could go in and ask him."

"Would you?"

"Sure."

"Thanks." Brooke headed in. "Brooke," Celia said, stopping her. "I'm sorry for how awful I was to you last year. I was wrong. I acted like a jerk."

"It's okay." Brooke smiled. "We're older now."

Late, late that night, there was post prom partying at the Bubble Café. It was after two and

114

there was hardly a table that wasn't crowded with Redwood High seniors. The floor was scattered with new high heels and polished patent leathers; rented tux jackets hung on the wooden chairs, and a few droopy corsages sat next to the burger baskets and vanilla malts.

Allie, Sean, and Brooke were at a tiny table up front, leaning on their elbows and picking over what was left of heaping platters of french fries and onion rings.

"I can't believe Derek was supposed to take Celia," Allie was saying, waving a soggy fry. "How was I supposed to know? This is so strange."

"Strange," Sean echoed, squeezing on more ketchup. "Sick is more like it."

"He must be a first-degree creep," Brooke yawned.

"Is he ever." Allie munched. "You should have seen him when we went to his dumb frat house afterward. First, he wouldn't keep his hands off me. Then he kept telling everybody I was already going to acting school in San Francisco. He wouldn't admit to anyone that we'd just been to my prom. I'm sure he was trying to make them all think I was a college girl. And then he got really mad when I told him to drop me off here instead of home. No way was I letting him try to slobber all over me on that dark road in front of my house. Puke city."

Brooke giggled.

Sean frowned. "Is that how you talk about guys when we're not around?"

Brooke kissed him. "Not you."

Allie leaned back and sighed. "I feel so awful, though. I know it wasn't my fault, but I still feel terrible. Poor Celia. No matter how much bizarre stuff she's done, she doesn't deserve this."

"She was going to walk home alone, at nine o'clock in that gorgeous dress, all the way across town," said Brooke. "It's a good thing Nick wanted to leave, too. I was ready to drive her home myself."

Sean nabbed the last onion ring. "I wonder why Nick wanted to go. He looked like he was having a good time."

"Not when I saw him. He seemed overjoyed to have an excuse to split."

"Weird," Sean and Allie responded at the same time.

"What a night," Allie sighed.

"Hey," Sean objected, smiling at Brooke. "We had a great time."

Allie rolled her eyes and fought him for the last fry. "I'm glad somebody did."

CHAPTER 11

It was nearly summer, but nothing felt summery. Instead of the smell of suntan lotion and rubber thongs between the toes, it was flat soda and wet socks. A sad song playing over and over. Sitting alone in the car while the rest of the world was a big beach party.

That was how the end of high school felt to Meg. It was finals week — the very final finals week, everybody kept saying. Then they'd laugh and go on about senior cut day and the principal mispronouncing names at graduation and how no one could graduate who had an outstanding library fine. Graduation was in twelve days and the Class of '88 had gone beyond senioritis and into some kind of crazy delirium. Except Meg. Meg still felt like she was caught in senior slump.

She'd finished her French exam a few minutes early and was waiting by her locker for Patrick. Even under the eaves where she stood, she could feel the three o'clock sun. The roses across the way were in full bloom now, and every time the breeze blew the aroma wafted over. But the light and the perfume and the warmth only reached Meg's eyes and nose and skin. Nothing soaked in any deeper.

The final bell rang, and the hall was cluttered with motion and noise. Patrick spotted Meg as soon as he left his room across the way. His cowboy boots scuffed the grass. The sun glimmered off his long hair, but his eyes were as dull and lifeless as Meg felt inside.

"How'd it go?" she asked him.

"Not too bad. One more day of finals over and done with. How about you?"

"Piece of cake."

They leaned against the metal doors, not sure what else to say. It had been like that since the prom two weeks ago. So much to say. Nobody saying anything. Even though Patrick couldn't know about Nick, he had to sense that something had changed. How could he not sense it? Since the prom Meg had been like a piece of plastic melted by the summer heat.

Patrick shifted so a bashful sophomore could get to the locker behind him. "They need people to hand out programs for the talent show next Monday. I signed you up. Is that okay?"

"Sure."

"I couldn't find you after lunch to ask you. Everybody's doing something. Sean's picking up the PA this afternoon. Maria's going to do refreshments. Celia's helping with costumes. If you really don't want to, though, I could take you off the list."

"No. It's fine."

"You sure?'

"I'll be there anyway to see Allie in the skit. I don't mind."

"Really?"

"Patrick, I want to."

"Okay." Patrick paused. "Joanne also asked if you and I could get downtown early on grad night to help set up signs and stuff. I told her I'd let her know." He picked a campaign flyer off the ground. It promoted some junior for next year's student body president. Patrick slowly crumpled it. "That is, if we're still going together . . . to grad night, I mean."

"Grad night?"

"Yeah. Are we? Still going to grad night together?"

"Of course."

"Good."

Meg looked away, feeling like the world's biggest hypocrite. But she'd thought about this whole mess long and hard and she'd decided. Patrick would probably go to Cornell. He hadn't made his final decision yet, but he had to go. Cornell was where he really wanted to study, and the university had gone on to offer him a scholarship and a slot in their summer school. Cornell didn't just accept Patrick, they wanted him! He'd be a fool to turn them down.

So, that meant that she and Patrick would be separated soon. Naturally. Gracefully. And from there they would just drift apart. She knew now that she couldn't stay with Patrick, but to break up right before graduation seemed so mean and unfair. She'd stick by him until he left for Cornell. That was best. There was no other way.

"Did you see this?" Patrick asked, pulling a newspaper out of his horticulture textbook.

Meg flinched. It was the latest issue of *The Guardian*. She didn't want to see Nick's words right now or even his name. But then she remembered that his farewell article had been printed the previous week. She took the paper.

"It's a special senior issue."

Meg leafed through it and saw that all the articles were on grad night, the talent show, and senior award winners. There was that silly "I Will and Bequeath" list they printed every year. Sam Pond left his hair to science. Greg Kendall left his unmentionables to Sam Pond. Deb Dryden willed her old gym clothes to Jim Edmundson, and Sean bequeathed his favorite Bronski Beat album to Mr. Thorson.

But toward the bottom, between Joanne willing happiness and success to the Class of '89 and Phil Davidson leaving his body and looks to himself, was a short bequest that caught Meg's heart. *From N.R. to Lightning: I will and bequeath my fastest pair of track shoes, my game of Clue, and so much more.*

A secret message from Nick. Who else could know that she and Nick used to spend hours up in the old tree house in his backyard playing Clue with Sean, Celia, or Allie. Who else had raced her countless times up and down Capitola Mountain until he nicknamed her "Lightning."

The blood rushed to Meg's face. Since the prom she'd only spoken to Nick once — once to say, *We can't be together now. I'm still with Patrick. Maybe once Patrick is away, I can tell him I'm going to date other people, and we can start to figure things out. But for now, we have to keep our distance.* Since then, they sat in the same classrooms, passed each other in the halls, and didn't say a word. They didn't smile or even wave. And yet every time she saw Nick, every inch of her body was tuned to nothing but him.

"What are you reading?"

"Nothing," Meg gasped, slapping the paper closed. "Those dumb will and bequeath things." She turned and blindly rifled through her locker. She had no idea what she was looking for.

"Listen, I have to go to that senior awards rehearsal now," Patrick said. He was receiving an achievement award from the Rotary Club. "But I wanted to tell you that I finally made a decision about Cornell."

Meg felt her first hint of relief since the prom. Leaving her locker open, she turned to look at Patrick's sweet, handsome face and knew she was handling this in the best way. She was right not to tell him about Nick. Patrick was the last guy in the world who deserved to be dumped. "You're going," Meg breathed happily. "You should, you know. It's the right place for you."

He looked hurt. "You mean Cornell?"

"Yes."

"Actually, I'm going to Berkeley. That's what I wanted to tell you."

Meg was stunned. "You're going to Berkeley?"

Patrick nodded defiantly.

"Patrick, why?"

"Why not?" he came back with a little anger.

"I don't know." Meg rested her face in her hands and took a deep breath. She summoned all her courage and said, "Just as long as you're not going there for me. Don't do that, Patrick. It's too important. College is too important for that."

"Who says I'm doing it for you?" Patrick objected. He got angry so infrequently that it hit Meg like a punch in the stomach. "It has nothing to do with you. I'm going to Berkeley because that's where I want to go!"

"Okay. I'm sorry. Patrick, don't get upset."

"I'm not upset!"

"All right."

They stood silently. Finally Meg put her arm around his shoulder and kissed his cheek. He didn't move.

"Aren't you glad?" Patrick said.

Meg let go and smiled. She couldn't say anything, but at least she nodded and smiled. Then she went back to rifling through her locker.

"Well, I guess I should go to that meeting. Should I call you tonight?"

"If you want."

"What time?"

"Any time. It doesn't matter." Suddenly Meg threw her French book into her locker. It whacked the metal wall, then tumbled to the concrete. Patrick turned back. She shook her head and let out a long, heavy sigh. "Patrick," she heaved, biting back her frustration. "Remember when we were freshmen and the school was brand-new?"

"Of course."

"Do you remember how the lockers looked then? How the paint was so perfect and shiny?" Patrick nodded. He picked up her book and placed it inside. Her locker was already half cleaned out. No more pictures or track gear. Lab manuals and library books had been turned in. All that was left were a senior events calendar, two textbooks, scratches, and a patch of rust. "I don't know why I thought about that all of a sudden, but I did."

"Everything in the world seemed new then," Patrick said.

"Yes." Meg slowly closed the door and looked down the walkway. There was a mural painted by the Class of '85, trash cans decorated by the Class of '87, the concrete was cracked in a few places, and there was a big black spot where some kid had lit a bonfire when Meg was a sophomore. She sighed. "Hey, how about if I walk you over to your meeting."

"I'd like that." He reached for her hand and held it tightly. "Let's go."

"NOT AGAIN!"

Sean turned left — abruptly — and deliberately drove around the block. He wasn't going to do it . . . he wasn't, he wasn't, he wasn't! The lady in the car right behind him slammed on her brakes.

She rolled down her window. "ARE YOU CRAZY?" she yelled.

Sean had been signaling a right turn for two blocks and then he went the other way. Well, sorry lady. I'm feeling a little erratic this afternoon. In fact I'm feeling downright berserko. I've got to go and rent another piece of equipment from Jay "Dreary" Creary, a fate worse than watching reruns of eighth-grade health movies.

The lady accelerated and left Sean in her dust. Okay, so he wasn't being the driver of the year, and maybe if he kept going this way his dad's insurance rates would go up, but if the van was acting the way Sean felt, then the speedometer would be going round and round like a cuckoo clock and the rearview mirror would be spinning like the rotor on a helicopter.

"URRAAHHHHHH!" Sean yelled.

He pounded the dashboard, but he could only avoid it so long. He'd volunteered — *volunteered* — to rent the PA speakers for the talent show. He'd thought that he could get the stuff at Kimbel Sound, a professional rock musicians' store and hangout. Well, it had turned out that everybody in Redwood Hills needed a PA system that week and Kimbel's was out. Who do they recommend? — Payson's Stereo. Home of the good sound of innumerable superb stereo components and the bad, bad sound of Jay Cleary.

Just thinking of Jay's laugh and that fleshy

124

face made Sean pull over and slam on his brakes. Jay was going to humiliate him again, make him relive all the things as a freshman that he'd just taken the last three years of high school to get over. But what could he do? He had to get the PA, and seeing Jay again was probably better than putting the driving public in jeopardy. Maybe. Sean accelerated, and when he came around and got to the corner again, he turned right like he was supposed to.

The store was waiting. Low, squat, with big posters in the window. Sean could tell as soon as he walked across the mall that there were lots of people in there, too. Great, he was going to be humiliated in front of the stereo-buying masses. Jay was going to remind Sean of every zit he ever had on his chin, every time his voice cracked, every dumb thing he ever said or did as a freshman. It was like going back into a nightmare.

Sean pushed open the front door. A little bell rang. The cool air was clean and tasteless, and only rack after rack of glowing electronic lights made Sean feel welcome.

"Hello."

"Hi."

"Can I help you?" It wasn't Jay, but an older guy with a beard and glasses wearing a sports coat and tie.

"I need to rent some PA speakers. The people over at Kimbel's said you might have some."

"We do," the man responded. He went behind the counter as Sean kept his eyes peeled, waiting to be ambushed any second by Jay.

"It's for Redwood High," Sean explained, following. He wanted to avoid getting stuck there answering questions about deposits and ID.

Suddenly the guy looked up. His smile disappeared and he leaned over the counter. "Did you rent from us a few weeks ago?"

"Uh, yes. I guess I did."

"Are you the fellow that fixed that V.U. meter on the tape recorder?"

Uh-oh, Sean thought. Here it comes. Jay's laid out the welcome wagon. "That was me," Sean mumbled.

"Well, you did a terrific job."

"I did?"

"Yes, I was very impressed." He stuck out his hand to shake. "I'm Herman Payson. You must have studied electronics."

"A little," Sean admitted, not quite sure if this was real or if Jay was about to jump up from behind the counter and go "booga-booga." "It's sort of my hobby, too."

"Well, you did a first-rate job. I should apologize for renting out a broken piece of equipment in the first place. How about if I loan you the speakers without charge. Will that make up for it?"

Sean couldn't believe it. He looked around at the other people talking to the salesmen and wondered if he'd gone into the wrong store. "Well, sure."

"Let's see. Who helped you when you returned the recorder? I'll have to get the receipt and put it together with this one."

"You mean who the salesman was?"

"Mmm."

126

Sean gulped. "Jay."

"Who?"

"Jay. Jay Creary."

Mr. Payson looked confused. "The big blond kid?"

"Yeah. Jay."

"The one who always wears the letter jacket, no matter how hot it is outside."

Sean shrugged.

Finally Mr. Payson found the receipt and read it. He took off his glasses, squinted, and read it again. "Did he tell you he was a salesman?"

"Isn't he?"

Mr. Payson put his glasses back on and shook his head. "He's not supposed to get near any of our stock. Except to dust it off. He's the night janitor."

Sean suddenly felt dizzy. This was crazier than driving the car around the block umpteen times. This was going off the road, although Sean had never gone off the road and he didn't want to start now, but everything seemed to be turned upside down. "Jay is the janitor?" he finally managed.

"Sometimes I wonder if I should even let him do that. He's been here since he flunked out of college last year. It's a little pathetic."

"What?"

"That jacket. It's his old high school jacket with a fake college letter stuck on. He never even made the college team. He never takes it off. That kid is a real loser." Payson waved the receipt. "He's going to get a talking-to about this, that's for sure."

Payson called behind the counter to another

guy about fetching Sean's PA speakers. Sean was so shell-shocked that they could have brought up a VCR, and he wouldn't have known the difference. He signed the receipt and thanked the guy and showed the assistant where his van was parked. They loaded the speakers in the back, and then Sean got his keys and went up front. It took him about five minutes to unlock the door. All he could think about was Jay Creary was a loser ... Jay Creary was a phony ... until finally, slowly, another thought entered his mind.

Revenge. It was time. Revenge.

CHAPTER 12

"Back in the days of the Stone Age, there was an early species of man called freshman," Allie projected. She waited. "CALLED FRESH-MAN," she pronounced again. Finally she cleared her throat, cupped her hands over her mouth and prompted loudly, "FRESHMANNN."

"Hold it, Al. I think we have a problem."

Allie looked down from the lip of the stage into the almost-empty auditorium. Her fellow talent show performers were giggling and even Ms. Smith, the drama teacher, was stifling laughter. When Allie finally turned around to look she broke up, too. There was Brooke, with Sean and Penny Hewitt, way upstage, fumbling with a huge cardboard dinosaur. The dinosaur was mounted on a little cart that had overturned, and all three of them looked like they were in a Stone Age wrestling match.

"Sorry you didn't get your music cue, Al,"

Sean said, looking up and sweating. "But I had to leave the sound board. The girls looked like they needed some caveman help."

Brooke rolled her eyes and teased. "Watch it, Sean. This happens to be a female dinosaur."

"Excuse me," he grinned, springing his hands away.

Allie was almost sorry she'd come up with this idea. The talent show was called The History of High School Man. Allie'd suggested using a few background pieces, like the cardboard dinosaur, to represent progress through the years. To begin, Sean would play the theme from *2001*, and the dinosaur would slide out. Then Allie would pat its head and start her dialogue. She would play a time traveler, who went from freshman year to the present, interacting with life along the way and interpreting it for the audience.

"We need a few minutes," Brooke requested, pulling some nails out of her overalls and checking the bottom of the cart. "We have to do some dino-repair."

"Okay." Ms. Smith stood up and clapped her hands. "Everybody take a ten-minute break."

The rehearsal became instant chaos. Four kids jumped up for extra practice on the last part of the skit, the senior sketch, which began as a circus. They called it circus senioritis. It was sort of a free-for-all where Bob Barnett juggled, Sally Ann Stormis circled around on roller skates, Sam Pond walked on his hands, and Dan Kremer did a rap song. The four of them took over the front of the stage while Terry McMahan

130

went out for doughnuts, and Ursula West went over her dance solo in the aisle.

Allie hopped down from the stage and headed for the lobby to go over her lines. Once through the double doors she sat on the cool linoleum and murmured to herself.

"Good-bye to laps around the field and tardy bells," Allie said, "dress codes and cafeteria food. Farewell to the quad in spring, to Ms. Smith, to summer vacation, and Mr. McClure writing TGIF on his board every Friday."

Those were her lines for the very end of the talent show, where she had made it to the present and was going on to face the future. Allie'd written this part herself, patterning it after the last act of *Our Town*, the play she'd had the lead in a year ago. Every time she'd come to the end of *Our Town*, her voice had caught and her eyes had filled up. Now, just going over the words for the talent show, she was starting to have the same reaction.

"You are such a wimp," she told herself, leaning back against the wall and closing her eyes.

This was silly. She was being overly emotional again, dramatic with a capital D, as her father liked to say. The wave of feeling ceased, but when she opened her eyes again she saw the lobby door crack open and Celia's face peek in. Allie looked right at her ex-best friend. She wasn't sure what Celia was doing there, or if she should even talk to her.

Celia held herself stiffly, as if she were encased in thin ice. She stayed in the doorway and held up a little paper sack. "Hi."

131

"Hi, Celia." Allie hadn't seen Celia since she'd found out about Derek and the prom.

"I'm supposed to be helping with the costumes for the talent show," Celia rambled quickly. She pulled a Butterick pattern out of the sack. "I thought you could wear this." She took two steps in and flashed the pattern in front of Allie, a simple jumper. "Mrs. Thone in home ec said she could make it up really fast. It's plain so you can layer stuff on top of it to change for the different years. Does that sound okay?"

Allie stared at her. Celia was so pretty. Ever since Allie had known her she had looked perfect — never awkward or scuzzy or wrong. And yet as she grew older and even more beautiful, Allie started to notice an aloofness, a guardedness hiding those lovely features that made her less attractive than a more ordinary-looking girl like Brooke. But at that moment, holding the pattern up, the guardedness had a crack in it.

"That sounds fine. Thanks."

Celia backed up. "Mrs. Thone wants you to stop by her room sometime in the next few days to make sure it fits."

"All right." Celia started to go but stopped when Allie called back to her.

"Cici. Um, Cici, I didn't know about it, you know."

Celia turned around. "About what?" she asked without emotion.

"About Derek. That he was your boyfriend."

"He wasn't my boyfriend," Celia came right back, her eyes meeting Allie's. "I just went out

132

with him a few times. He's free to date whoever he wants."

"Celia, he was supposed to take you to the prom."

Celia winced slightly, and Allie wished she'd kept her big mouth shut or at least had rearranged the words in a different way. She tried again. "Um, I know that now — not that everybody does. I'm just trying to say I didn't know then. I would never have done that to you. You understand that?"

"That's what Brooke said," Celia admitted, finally showing a hint of softness. Just as quickly, she stiffened again. "It doesn't matter anymore. I hope you and Derek will be very happy together." She started to go. The coolness had come back.

"Cici!"

Allie suddenly wanted to grab Celia, to shake her and scream at the top of her lungs, anything to get to the real Celia, the Celia that could admit that, yes, it hurt. Lots of things hurt. It hurt to get dumped. Just like it hurt when they severed their friendship a year ago. And it hurt when Celia snubbed Brooke, and when Allie came back from New York and didn't know where she fit in anymore. Life was bound to have a lot more hurt in store for them — Allie probably knew that better than any of them. But she also knew that if they pretended that the hurt wasn't there — if they just ignored it — then it might never go away.

"Cici, wait," Allie said again.

Celia came back into the lobby and plastered herself against the door, as if she was afraid that someone else might come in and overhear. "What?"

"You are such a jerk sometimes," Allie provoked, desperate for a reaction.

Celia's cheeks started to redden and her mouth dropped open. "What did you say?"

"You heard me. You're a jerk."

"I'm a jerk?"

Allie went in for the kill. "Yes. You are a snob and a fool and an incredible jerk."

"Oh, I love this," Celia started to seethe. "This is great. I'm a jerk! You show up at the prom with my date and I'm a jerk. You reject me last year after I did everything I could to help you when you were in trouble, when nobody else even wanted to talk to you. And you have the nerve to tell me that I'm a jerk!"

"That's right."

"Well," Celia ranted, finally losing control. "I'll tell you what I think. I think that you're the jerk. Just because I made some mistakes. Just because I did the wrong thing when you came back from New York. Just because I made a mistake about Brooke, you are never going to let me forget it. No, you won't ever be my friend again no matter how much I miss you. Because you're so happy and successful and you don't need me anymore. Well, I don't need you, either. Or Sean. Do you hear me? I don't need any of you!"

Allie suddenly started to laugh. She had no idea why she was laughing, but there was something wonderful about seeing Celia, after all this time, explode at the seams in front of her.

"What are you laughing at!" Celia demanded, getting even more enraged.

"You," Allie giggled, starting to go off on one of her wild laughing jags. "Me. Us fighting about something we should have cleared up so long ago. And do you know what's the funniest?"

"What."

Allie laughed even harder. "Us fighting about that creep, Derek."

Celia pouted, still furious. "At least that's one thing we agree on."

Allie walked over to her. She suddenly knew that she had nothing to lose. There was nothing worse or more painful that could happen between her and Celia than what had happened already. With great daring, she threw her arms around Celia and hugged her. She felt Celia's slender limbs stiffen. She ignored it. She plunged ahead.

"Of course he's a creep," Allie sighed. "And believe me, I'm not going back for more."

She hung on tight. There was a slight trembling and then she felt Celia's head fall, plop, right onto her shoulder. Celia's back started to shake and there were tiny muffled gasps, and Allie knew that she was crying. "It's okay, Cici. It's okay." Allie held her tightly until she calmed.

Celia pulled away, sniffling. She looked embarrassed but too exposed to try and cover her feelings any longer. "God, I'm crying a lot lately," she said, trying to regain control. "It's pathetic. Do you think all seniors do this?"

Allie smiled, totally dry-eyed. "Probably. But you know me. I've been a crybaby from day one."

"That's for sure."

Allie backed up and put her hands on her hips. "Hey, thanks a lot."

"Well," Celia said, wiping away her tears and starting to smile. "If you can tell me I'm a jerk, I can tell you that you are an impossible, overly emotional nut case!"

They glared at each other and almost at the same time burst out laughing.

"It's true," Allie giggled hopelessly. "I'm a nut case."

Celia took a deep breath. "And I'm a fool," she finally breathed.

"No."

They both stood quietly. They could hear Sean testing the sound levels inside the auditorium, Bob's juggling balls thunking to the floor, and Ms. Smith yelling for Sally Ann to be careful on her skates.

"I've really missed you, Al," Celia said finally.

"Yeah," Allie responded. "There is something about old friends, isn't there?"

"There is."

"So do you forgive me about Derek?" Allie asked. "I really didn't know."

"How could you know," Celia sighed sadly. "We barely talk to each other anymore." She played with lace on the hem of her sundress, then looked up. "I don't even know what you're doing next year. Are you going to be around here?"

"Probably. I got accepted to this acting school in San Francisco — "

"Al, that's fantastic!"

Allie held up her hands. "Not really. My dad refuses to pay for it. He's never come to see me act, but he's sure that's not what I should do with my life."

"He hasn't come to see any of your plays?"

"Not one."

"I don't believe that."

"Believe it. Anyway, he wants me to live at home and go to Redwood College. If I can't get a job and make enough money to support myself, I guess that's what I'll end up doing."

"Well, at least we could see each other then. I'm going to Redwood. Business major. And living at home, of course. The dorms are too expensive."

Allie nodded.

They heard quick footsteps and both turned to see the double doors open. Brooke stuck her head in. She looked surprised to see Celia there. "Hi, Celia."

"Hi."

"We fixed Mr. T. Rex. At least I hope we did. Come on, Al. We're ready to try it again." Brooke smiled at Celia and went back into the auditorium.

"Why don't you stay and watch for a while," Allie invited. "It's pretty funny."

"Do you mind?'

"I'd like it. Come on."

"Okay."

They went through the doors and started up the aisle. Bob was onstage, pitching his juggling balls to Sam Pond, who was walking upside down and catching them with his feet. Allie and Celia paused for a moment to watch.

"Off the stage, boys," Ms. Smith commanded. "Let's go, Al."

Allie hesitated. "Celia, we're going to the Bubble after rehearsal to get something to eat. Do you want to come?"

Celia gave a soft smile. "Sure. Thanks."

"Sean's driving. And Brooke's coming, too." Allie stared at Celia hard, testing her. No matter how badly she wanted to be friends again, she wouldn't do it at Brooke's expense.

Celia looked up at Brooke, who was back on stage in her overalls, kneeling and pounding something into the dinosaur's feet. Celia smiled. "That's okay." She looked a little embarrassed. "Actually, it's better than okay," she backtracked. "Its great."

"You mean it?"

Celia nodded. "Now go on, get up there. I want to see what you do with that dumb dinosaur."

Allie grinned and then, with both hands, boosted herself up on stage. When she turned around, Celia was sitting front row center and waiting, with a smile on her face, for things to happen.

CHAPTER 13

Six days left. Six.

That was all Nick could think about as he jogged up Capitola Mountain. He timed his breathing in sixes. His feet made six puffs of dirt before starting over and making six again. It seemed like Hughie, who panted and ran next to him, had stopped to bark and sniff six times. If it wasn't so hot Nick might have run six miles or jogged the steepest slope six more times or kept going until six o'clock.

But it was hot. Dry, dusty hot. He was probably a fool to run at all in this heat but his parents were at it again, and he didn't want to deal with Celia or his aunt right now. Everything inside him now was so roped up that to untie any of it seemed impossible.

"Hey, Hugh. What are you doing? C'mon, don't be a knothead."

Hughie was barking again and pointing. He

had that nutty look he got whenever there was a pheasant or a quail within sniffing range. Nick had never actually seen one of those birds himself, but he'd heard that they were up here, and Hughie certainly seemed to think so. Sure enough, Hughie left the trail and made a beeline into the woods.

"HUGHIE," Nick ordered, "COME BACK HERE." Hughie's bark shrank into the distance. Nick stopped and slapped his thigh. "Hugh, it's too hot for this," he muttered to himself.

Then Nick heard a silvery laugh and a voice from the trail on the other side of the thicket. "Hugh! Hi, Hughie," the girl cooed. "Yes. Yes. What are you doing out here?"

Nick knew the voice instantly. He crouched down on the trail, his strong legs suddenly wobbling beneath him. "Meg."

There was Hughie's quick trampling, then the slower, louder swishes of Meg parting branches and kicking dried leaves. Soon she appeared, ducking the branch of an old oak, wearing track shorts and a sleeveless T-shirt. Her hair was braided and her face flushed.

Nick stared. He wanted to run to her, to tackle her to the ground. Both of them in that lush bed of leaves. But he couldn't. Just like with his parents, his feelings for Meg had to be shoved down, hidden, tied up tight.

"Hi," Meg said, petting Hughie's head and trying to look surprised.

Nick knew she wasn't surprised. Hughie rarely went out of the yard by himself, let alone all the way up here. "Hi." Nick snapped his fingers.

"Come on, Hugh. Leave her alone. Let her go on with her run." Hughie trotted over and sat down next to him. Meg stayed.

"How are you?" she asked, leaning back against a tree. Her legs were deeply tanned and loose strands of hair were plastered to her neck. Nick couldn't take his eyes off her.

"Okay. You?"

"Fair. I saw the will and bequeath you left me in the paper."

"You did?"

"Thanks." She looked away.

"So you're only doing fair?"

She nodded.

"How's Patrick?"

The brightness left her face. "I don't think he knows anything. It's been hard, though. He's turning down Cornell. He's going to Berkeley. He told me on Tuesday."

"What did you say?"

"Me?"

"Meg!"

"What do you mean?"

"Meg, you know he's going to Berkeley so he can be with you!" Nick's anger erupted so suddenly it surprised even him. "Didn't you tell him anything?"

She looked a little scared. "Tell him what?"

He shot to his feet, making Hughie whimper and scuttle back. "About us!"

"What about us, Nick? Things have never worked out with us. What makes you think they will now?"

"Well, then how about how you feel about

him! Do you love him? Do you want to spend your college years with him?"

Meg didn't answer.

"DO YOU?"

"No," Meg finally said, very softly.

"What is this?!" Nick exploded. "Are we all waiting for graduation so we can stop lying to each other? I'm not sure how that's going to change anything, but we'd better hurry up, because we've only got six more days. Think about it, Meg, six more days!" He was next to her now and grabbing her arms, holding her so tightly his fingers left white marks when he let go. "You're as bad as my parents," he said disgustedly. "We both are."

They stood apart while a butterfly hovered and a squirrel skittered by.

"What do you mean about your parents?"

There no longer seemed any point in holding back, especially with Meg. "They're fighting all the time. It's been like this since last summer. They yell at each other for yelling so loud that I can hear it. And then when they see me, they put on this act like everything is just perfect. It's making me crazy."

"Have you talked to them about it? Told them you know what's going on?"

"What's the point?"

"I don't know. At least then things would be out in the open, you'd know where you stand. You should tell them, Nick."

"Just like you're going to tell Patrick?"

She closed her eyes in pain and leaned her

142

head back against the tree. "What are we going to do?"

Nick walked over to her. He rested his hand on the tree trunk behind her, and the next thing he knew they were kissing. Hot, damp skin, bare arms and legs touching, quick breathing and her holding him so tightly. He was so dizzy when he pulled back that the patchy sky twirled like a kaleidoscope.

"I just know I love you," he was barely able to say.

"I love you, too." She pried herself away. "But it may not make any difference."

He let her go. She headed back onto the trail. Hughie followed for a few feet, then trotted back when he realized that Nick wasn't joining her.

"Will you talk to them, Nick?" she asked. Her cheeks were even redder than they had been from running. Her eyes looked frightened and confused.

"I don't know. How about you and Patrick?"

"I want to." She slowly began walking. "I just don't know if I can."

He stared after her until even the sound of her footsteps was gone.

"What will you do if you see Derek, if he comes into the café tonight, I mean?"

Celia thought for a moment. "I'll pour hot coffee down his pipe."

Allie and Brooke howled with laughter.

"No, seriously."

Celia leaned forward on the car seat and grinned. "Who said I was kidding?"

The three girls had just finished the last talent show rehearsal before the big event on Monday. Brooke had offered to drive Celia to her waitress job, and Celia had gratefully accepted. They were trying to get through the downtown five o'clock traffic so they could get her to the Redwood campus on time.

"This last poem he sent me was the pukiest," Allie giggled. "He knows I was mad at him after the prom, so he keeps sending me these dumb poems. I don't think he has the nerve to call me on the phone."

"No, it's that he thinks he's such a whiz poet." Celia stuck her head out the car window and screamed. "AAAAAUGGGGGHHH!"

"I think his poems are a riot," Brooke offered, smiling at Celia in the rearview mirror. "Al, read Celia the latest one. Celia, you won't believe this."

Allie turned back. "You don't really want to hear this do you?"

Celia nodded. "Read it. Then I'll show you some of mine. He probably recycled the worst ones."

"Okay." Allie dug in her bag. She unfolded the sheet of legal paper, read it once to herself, and burst out laughing.

"Al, come on. Don't keep the good parts to yourself."

Allie was on the verge of one of her famous laughing jags, but she gulped back some air and forced herself to read. "Sorry. Here goes." She cleared her throat.

star crossed
star wars
starring *****
YOU
            me

she's flashy
not a flash in the pan
electric
but not wired
hot
but not burned out

on saturday
on frat row
on my turf *****
US
            be there

"THAT'S AAAAWWWWFULLL!!" all three
cried at the same time. Allie laughed endlessly
and flapped her hands while Celia pounded on the
car seat and Brooke wiped her eyes.

"Oh, you guys, we can't have this much fun,"
Brooke sighed, "I'll get us in a wreck."

"Wait a minute. I remember that open house
party!" Celia said suddenly. "It's this big deal on
frat row. It's tomorrow, starting in the afternoon
and going almost all night. Derek wanted me to
go with him, before . . . before. . . ." Her voice
trailed off.

"Before he showed himself to be a total slimebucket," Brooke finished for her.

Celia smiled again. "That's exactly what I was

going to say." She looked out the window. The
traffic was moving again, and the Redwood College campus was coming into view. "I guess it
was really slimy of him to dump me just because
my mom is the way she is. It's not my fault. Besides, she's not *that* bad."

"Your mom is great," Allie said. They were
quiet until Allie suddenly turned back again. "Do
you really think Derek dumped you because of
your mom? I mean, he's a sleaze, but I thought
he kind of liked funky types. He really tried to
impress the drama crowd at the prom. I think
that's what he saw in me."

"Al, I'm sure. We were with his dumb frat
brothers at the café, right after he asked me to the
prom, and then my mom came in and he just
turned off. Like that."

Allie was hanging so far over her seat now she
was practically falling in Celia's lap. "Wait a
second. Did you mention the prom or high school
around the other guys?"

"I don't know. Probably."

"Because, Cici, that's what he's freaked out
about. He was with me, anyway. I mean, he
doesn't want his frat buddies to know that he's
dating girls in high school. I'm sure of it."

"Really?"

"I'm positive."

Celia sat back and pensively put her hand to
her mouth. "Now that I think about it, that does
kind of make sense. Why did I assume it was my
mom?"

Allie shrugged. "You always did like to blame

stuff on her." She touched Celia's knee. "No offense."

"No." Celia stared out the window, absorbed in thought.

Allie went on. "Anyway, I think we should figure out some way to pay him back. That is so selfish and creepy — the way he lied to both of us."

"What could we do, though?" added Brooke, steering her old Rambler into the campus parking lot. She laughed. "We could make him read his own poetry."

Celia shook her head. "He does that already. There's nothing that makes him happier."

They all groaned.

"We could. . . ." Allie paused to brainstorm. "I know! Celia and I could both show up at the frat party as his dates."

"Wait a second," Celia gasped, her blue-green eyes getting big and bright. "How about if it was all three of us." As Brooke parked and plucked the key out of the ignition, she added, "I have an idea. You guys listen and tell me what you think."

Fifteen minutes later, Brooke was waiting outside Derek's poetry classroom. Celia'd had to go to work at the café, but Allie was with her, coaching and prodding.

"I'll never be able to do this, Al," Brooke said, burying her face in her hands.

"It's easy. Just pretend he's somebody else. Act like you're with Sean."

"Allie, you're the actress. I just build the sets."

"Here, wear this," Allie encouraged, taking off her man's vest and slipping it over Brooke's overalls. "This, too." Allie added her baseball cap, plastic belt, and glittery scarf. Brooke stood there like a little kid being dressed for the snow. "He's attracted to arty types."

Brooke looked down at herself and frowned. "I look ridiculous."

"You look great." Allie pulled a Redwood College paper binder out of her bag. "And hold this. It's my dad's. It'll make him think you're in college."

The classroom door was open a crack, and Allie pushed Brooke toward it. "I'll be outside in the quad. Good luck."

"Allie," Brooke whispered loudly as Allie was leaving, "this isn't going to work!" But Allie was gone. "Oh, no," Brooke groaned to herself. Then she rearranged her hat and scarf and belt, took a deep breath, and waited.

"I'll never pull this off," she muttered under her breath as she saw Derek appear in the hall. He stopped to light his pipe. She crossed her fingers, took a deep breath, and made her move. Quickly she made her way through the crowd until she stood next to him. She bumped his arm. "Sorry," she said loudly.

He looked up from his pipe, still holding the lit match between his fingers.

Brooke got up on her tiptoes and blew the match out. She almost giggled at her own daring but controlled herself when he looked right at her, surprised and pleased.

148

"Are you in O'Conner's poetry writing class?" she asked him.

He nodded and puffed.

"Because I was thinking of taking it next year, and I wanted to talk to somebody who was in it, see if they liked it."

He took a step in. Suddenly he stared hard.

Brooke panicked. What if he recognized her from the prom! They'd only met for a second, but he might remember. She combed her blonde bangs down over her eyebrows and peered up at him.

Whatever flicker of recognition Derek had experienced, it seemed to pass. He stopped staring and took her arm, pulling her out of the crowd, over to the empty doorway to another classroom.

"Hi, I'm Derek Jamison," he said.

"My name's Daphne," Brooke heard herself lie. Daphne was her little sister's name.

"Daphne. That's very poetic," Derek said seductively.

"Well, I'm really interested in poetry. That's why I want to know who the best professor is."

Derek was smiling at her, taking in every inch of her short hair, her freckled skin, Allie's accessories covering her lavender overalls. Brooke blushed. He took a step closer. She shielded herself with the Redwood College folder.

"Maybe we should go somewhere and talk about this," Derek said with growing confidence. "It's a little complicated to just give you a one-word answer here in the hall. Why don't we go over to my frat house and you can look at some of my poetry — that'll give you an idea of what O'Conner is into."

Brooke bit her lip. "Gee, I can't now. I have a late class."

He moved in very close, trapping her in the doorway. "Hey, what are you doing tomorrow?"

Brooke shrugged.

"Don't try and tell me you have plans for every single minute."

"I guess I don't."

"Great." He grinned. "There's an open house at my frat. It starts at two in the afternoon and lasts till dawn. Why don't you come? Maybe I can sneak you up to my room and show you my poems." He suddenly frowned and rubbed his forehead.

"What's the matter?" Brooke prompted. "Did you just remember something?"

"No. Nothing important. Just some other girl I told about the open house. It wasn't a real date or anything. She probably won't come anyway."

"Are you sure?"

"Nah. Who cares if she does." He nudged Brooke's shoulder. "So which dorm are you in?"

"You don't have to come get me," she responded, thinking fast. "Just tell me where and I'll meet you."

He looked skeptical. "Are you sure?"

She gloated. "I promise."

"That's great, babe. Great." He quickly scribbled the Sigma house number and ripped the paper out of his notepad. "Try and get there early."

"Okay."

He showed a split second of doubt. "You sure you'll be there?"

Brooke lovingly folded the paper and winked. "I'm sure."

He chucked her chin with his knuckles. She resisted the urge to punch him. "Look, babe, I have to go meet one of my frat brothers now, but I can't wait till tomorrow."

"Me, either," she said as she waved and watched him trot cockily down the other end of the hall. "Me, either."

After he was gone, she bolted into the quad and pulled Allie up from where she was lounging on the warm grass. Together they ran all the way to the Underground Café.

They plowed down the steps into the café and gestured to Celia, who was just finishing taking an order. Celia stuffed her order pad in her apron and rushed over to meet them.

"What happened?" Celia had to know.

"He fell for it," Allie panted.

"One hundred percent," nodded Brooke.

"THAT SLIMEBUCKET," all three of them said at the same time. Then they fell together, laughing.

CHAPTER 14

They said the heat wave had started again. The same parching heat wave Meg had endured for most of her eighteen years. Almost every June it turned so hot that she had to spray her sheets with ice water in order to fall asleep. Cantaloupe and lemon sherbet were the only things she felt like eating and there was no fuss deciding what to wear — she grabbed whatever was lightest and briefest and didn't stick to the small of her back.

"You feeling okay?" her mom asked, standing at the kitchen sink. She was digging seedlings from a long flat tray and transferring them to separate clay pots.

Meg was slumped over the table. An untouched sandwich sat in front of her. She stared out the window, past the porch swing and the potted plants at Sean's two-story house across the street. His parents' van, a few bicycles, and Brooke's old Rambler were parked in front. "I'm just tired."

"It's this heat."

Meg nodded, even though she knew it wasn't the heat at all. Since she'd met Nick in the woods yesterday, she'd decided. Nick was right. She had to tell Patrick the truth, even though just thinking about it made her want to crawl back under those clammy sheets. All night she'd primed herself, deciding what she would say, how he would react. She had to do it today. Otherwise, she would chicken out forever.

"Do you have plans for this afternoon?" Her mom washed her hands and pushed back her long graying hair. "It's almost one. It's not like you to just sit around."

"I guess. I thought I'd walk over to Patrick's."

"That's nice. You two doing anything special?"

"Not really."

"There still must be a lot to go over about graduation and everything. You have a very busy week coming up."

Meg felt queasy. "I know."

Her mom came over and touched her shoulder. "Honey, you don't look very enthusiastic. If you'd rather, you can stay here and keep me company in the basement." Meg's mom was a potter and had a studio downstairs. "Your dad's working all day, so I thought I'd make those bowls for the gift shop in the mall."

Meg squeezed her mother's hand. The basement. It was cool there and the sound of the potting wheel and the smell of the wet clay were soothing. "You wouldn't mind?"

"Are you kidding?" her mom laughed, until

her smile turned sad. "Pretty soon you won't be around here at all."

"I won't, will I," Meg echoed, almost to herself.

Her mom kissed the top of her head. "Patrick can wait. You'll see plenty of him next year." She went back to the sink and brought Meg two pots. "I'll tell you what — you put these outside for me. I'll set up downstairs. I bet I can get that order out of the way, and then we'll make something for your dorm room. How about that?"

Meg carried the pots out and squinted into the bright sun. She took one more look at the street — the messy flower beds in front of Celia's house, the Redwood trees and the vegetable gardens and the kids playing in the lawn sprinklers. Four more blocks like this and she'd be at Patrick's.

"Meg, honey, are you coming?" her mom called.

Meg hesitated. Finally she set the pots on the porch, went back inside, and headed down to the basement.

"We're really going through with this?"

"Consider it a dare."

"Great, Allie. That's like in sixth grade."

"Brooke, isn't that the point?"

"The point is to look like we're freshmen or in junior high or middle school," insisted Celia. "No, the real point is that we make this a frat party that Derek Jamison will never forget."

"That's right."

"Okay, okay. So what am I supposed to do?"

154

"Brooke, just dress like a nerd."

"I always dress like a nerd."

"You do not."

"HEY!" Sean finally shouted, waving his arms for their attention. The girls looked up. "Nothing like three girls who know what they're doing."

Brooke laughed and gave Sean a shove onto his bed. He toppled over like a tree. "Don't bug us. We're figuring it out."

Sean shook his head. "I'm so glad you asked for my help."

They were in his bedroom. Sean had gone into the reaches of his closet to supply them with what he called "geek clothes." They were things that he'd grown out of — and he'd grown out of a lot, fast. Plaid pants and short-sleeved shirts, a Camp Toonerville sweater, a Boy Scout cap. Allie said this stuff would be the finishing touches to make them look dopey and young. Sean wasn't sure exactly how he felt when Allie said it. Still, he was sympathetic to their cause. It seemed as if they were all out to get the bad guys together.

"Look! Look at this!" Allie said gleefully. She was holding up a yellow cowboy shirt with pearly buttons and a guitar embroidered on each shoulder. "This is so skinny. This would barely fit Gumby," she exulted. "Sean, when did you wear this?"

"Last year."

The girls screamed with laughter.

"Watch it. I might not let you have it."

"Oh, Sean," Celia said, going through the box. "These things are rags. How come your mom let you save them?"

"She said they were worth saving."

"For what?"

"Rags," Sean admitted.

The clothes were flying out of the box now. Allie was trying to find something to go with the cowboy shirt. Brooke was examining a pair of black jeans that looked narrow enough to work as drain pipes to a sink. Celia was more business-like — flinging the stuff out of the way that wouldn't work and using her critical eye to identify the winners.

"Remember, we can't be totally ridiculous," she reminded Brooke and Allie. "Otherwise we won't get past the front door."

"You really think we will get past the front door?" Brooke asked.

"You will. But what I worry about is what's going to happen after that."

"Sean. . . ."

"I'm not kidding." He pulled Brooke onto his lap. "Some of those frat guys are animals."

"We can take care of them. Remember, this is a mission of vengeance," Celia said.

"This is a mission of silliness," Allie insisted, jumping on Sean's bed, too, and giggling.

"I don't know," Sean said, looking at them and lacing his arms around Brooke. "It seems to me this might be one group of nerds getting vengeance on another."

Sean finally agreed to drive them over to the frat house. Allie said it would ruin the whole effect if one of them drove and proved that they were old enough to have a license. Sean thought that was taking things a little far, but he didn't mind acting as their big brother.

The girls were in the back of the van. Allie was wearing the infamous cowboy shirt, and somehow it looked even sillier on her than it ever had on Sean. Celia had a ponytail sprouting from the top of her head and a thick layer of lipstick that was supposed to smell like strawberries. Brooke had on Sean's Boy Scout cap and an old pin of Allie's that said DON'T MISS THE FRESH-MAN FUNDRAISER, YOU'LL HAVE A GHOST OF A TIME. In fact all the girls were acting so goofy and juvenile that Sean thought they could pass for gradeschoolers. There was enough gum chewing to remind him of a thousand cows.

But even the gum chewing quieted when they turned onto frat row. Sean pulled over. Across from them was a three-story Tudor-style house with lead-paned windows and gentle sloping eaves. They could see some movement inside and a few people chatting on the lawn and lots of cars lined along the street. The three girls looked at each other.

"This is it," said Celia.

Allie eyed the house. "Looks pretty tame."

"Don't let the outside fool you," Sean warned, kissing Brooke. "Be careful." They piled out of the van and he was gone. Their last link to the safe world of responsible, sensitive males was broken.

"Let's go." Together they skipped up the Sigma front steps and knocked on the door.

A burly guy wearing suspenders and a bow tie opened it. As soon as he did, the girls understood Sean's warning. A ferocious noise — rock music, laughter, and carrying on — was bottled up in the living room. The girls bobbed around to look, but all they could see from the doorway was an occasional flailing arm or leg and a few electric fans.

"What can I do for you young ladies?" the guy asked, eyeing them suspiciously.

Brooke and Allie shrunk back.

Celia took charge. "We're friends of Derek Jamison's, one of your members. He invited us."

He didn't look convinced. "Jamison invited you? What are your names?"

Now Celia seemed unsure, so Brooke stepped forward. "Tell him Daphne's here." The guy nodded and left.

As soon as the guy left, Celia and Allie turned to Brooke and said at the same time, *"Daphne?"*

Brooke grinned. "He likes those poetic types."

The guy quickly reappeared. He was scratching his head and still looked at them with narrowed eyes. "Okay," he shrugged. "Jamison is in there, past the living room. Do me a favor, though, and stay away from the keg in the kitchen."

Celia led the way until the noise was BLAST-ING. It was head-in-a-nutcracker time, and there were sweaty bodies bouncing up and down in this big room that was probably usually the living room. Now it was more like going through an earthquake.

"Hi, cutie," a voice screamed out, and then a pair of hairy arms were grabbing Brooke around the waist. She couldn't even see who they belonged to, and all three girls responded by desperately hacking away at them with their fists. Finally they broke him off and kept moving.

"Whew," Brooke said, a little shaken. "If it's like this now, I'd hate to be here at midnight."

"Stick together, that's all," Allie said confidently. Celia looked at her and smiled.

They snaked their way through the dancing couples, the guys drinking beer and leaning against the walls, looking them over. Finally they made it to what must have been a study. It was quieter and there were groups of twos and threes — most talking — although one couple was necking in the corner. They spotted Derek, holding a book and having an intense conversation with a guy Celia had met once at the café. Bruce somebody . . . some Sigma bigwig who was a junior or a senior. Celia headed straight for them and caught Bruce's eye. He frowned.

"Hey, girls, who let you in?" Bruce demanded as they came closer. He didn't recognize Celia.

"We're friends of Derek's," Celia said pointedly.

Derek looked up from his book, and the expression on his face made all three girls smile. His jaw went slack, his mustache wilted, and his eyes popped open like two sunflowers. The girls surrounded him.

"Hi, Derek," Celia squealed, taking his arm.

Allie nestled against him on the other side. "Derek, hi."

"Hi, Derek. It's me, Daphne," added Brooke with a wave and a wink.

159

Derek grabbed the bookcase behind him. He looked like he was about to pass out.

Bruce was staring back and forth between the girls and Derek, appalled. "Do you know these girls, Jamison?"

"Oh, he knows us," Celia insisted. "But I bet he doesn't know that we know each other."

"You do?" Derek croaked in half a voice. Bruce was looking more and more disgusted.

"Let's say we go to school together." Celia turned to Bruce. "High school. We're going to be sophomores next year." She looked back at Derek. "And we happen to be very good friends."

"You are?" Derek gulped.

"Hey, Jamison," Bruce interrupted gruffly. "Where do you get off inviting girls this young? Do you want to get our charter revoked? What do you think we are here, total cradle robbers?"

"No. No, I don't, Bruce."

"Well," said Allie, "if you really don't want us here, we'll go."

Bruce barely noticed her. He was pointing his finger and looming over Derek. "I'm serious, Jamison. There're enough kids here under twenty-one for us to get busted for that keg already. This is all we need. Don't you have a brain?"

Derek mumbled incoherently.

"Or can't you get anybody but a fifteen-year-old to pay attention to you? I knew we shouldn't have let you in here, Jamison. I knew it."

Celia, Allie, and Brooke linked arms as they watched Bruce get angrier and angrier while Derek pleaded and cowered until he was practically crawling into the bookshelf. Finally, Bruce

160

threatened something about putting Derek on trial at the next meeting and marched brusquely out. After Bruce left, Derek looked up at them like a puppy who had just been bashed with a rolled-up newspaper. "Thanks a lot," he muttered.

"Poor Derek," Allie said. "I can't imagine what you did to deserve it."

He glanced up at Celia, then looked away and covered his face. "They're going to put me on probation. I just know they are."

"Aw, that's too bad," Celia commented. "But think on the bright side, Derek. If you can't go to the parties here anymore, you can always go to dances at Redwood High!" She interlocked arms with Allie and Brooke, and the three of them proudly marched out.

Sean wanted to cram the old jeans down Jay Creary's throat.

He hadn't said anything to the girls — not even Brooke. They were engaged in some kind of frolic, a jolly game. But not him. He was after real revenge. Long lasting. Below the belt. As ugly as possible.

When he'd found the Levi's at the bottom of the box, he knew it was time. God knows why his mother had saved them. Maybe because she never knew why they were cut with the straight blade of Nick's army knife, or spotted with bits of heavy silver tape. They were the jeans he'd been wearing when Nick had cut him down. The jeans he'd had on when Jay and his buddies had taped him to the flagpole.

Sean had snuck the jeans into the glove com-

161

partment so the girls wouldn't see. But Jay would see. Jay would see plenty. Maybe Sean still wasn't able to beat Jay up, but he could do it with words. And the whole time he'd hold the ripped up jeans in Jay's thick face. Remember these, Sean would threaten. Well, look where it got you, moron. Now you're a stupid janitor in a fake letter jacket. A joke. A failure. A pathetic loser.

Sean parked by City Hall and stormed over to the mall, arriving just before closing time. He'd figured that was when Jay's shift started, just before everyone else went home. The more he thought about those old shredded Levi's, the more he remembered that awful night almost four years ago, the more he filled with bitterness and rage.

He moved faster, just pushing into the store at a few minutes to six. As soon as he did he saw the back of Jay's letter jacket behind the counter. There was a vacuum cleaner hose slung over one shoulder and a bottle of Windex in his hand. Jay was laughing at something. But this time his laugh didn't give Sean the shivers. It made him smirk. Not a happy smile, but a mean, tooth-clenched grimace.

Sean marched up and slapped the shredded jeans on the counter. He waited. But before he could get Jay's attention, an older man appeared from behind a stack of equipment and walked over. When he saw Sean's jeans, he adjusted his glasses and looked again. Sean gave a tiny self-conscious laugh, scooped up the Levi's, and tucked them back under his arm.

"Oh, hello again," the man said, coming closer and smiling at Sean. It was Mr. Payson. "You're not having any trouble with those PA speakers, are you?"

"No." Sean wasn't quite sure what to do when Payson sat down on a stool next to him, as if he wanted to stay and chat. Sean kept standing and clutching his jeans. "As far as I can tell, they're fine."

Payson stuck out his hand to shake. "Sean Pendleton. That's your name, isn't it? I looked on your receipt the other day."

Sean nodded and managed to shake Mr. Payson's hand. He craned his neck to get a look into the back room again. Jay was emptying wastebaskets. Sean told himself to be patient. "Yes, sir. And you're Mr. Payson."

"That's right. I'm glad you stopped by. I'd like to talk to you." Mr. Payson swiveled on his stool and called into the back room. "Jay, could you please bring us a couple of sodas from the fridge?" Jay disappeared, and Mr. Payson turned back to Sean. "Would you like a cold Pepsi? This heat is crazy."

"Sure. Thanks."

A moment later Jay appeared holding two frosty cans. He handed them to Mr. Payson, who gestured that he should give one to Sean. When Jay recognized Sean, he froze, refusing to let go of the can. His tiny eyes burned with indignation.

Payson took the soda out of Jay's hand. "Jay, you can go back to work."

Jay backed up, knocking into a cardboard display and a stack of cassette tapes. He straightened things up again and scurried into the back room.

Payson rubbed his forehead. "I don't have the

heart to fire him because I know he'll never get another job, but he drives me crazy sometimes." He and Sean thirstily gulped their sodas.

"You wanted to talk to me, sir?" Sean reminded him, still keeping his eye on Jay.

Payson nodded. "I've been thinking about you since I heard about how you fixed that tape machine. Are you still at Redwood High?"

"Graduating this week."

"What are you doing next year?"

"I'm going to Cal Tech. Studying engineering and electronics."

Payson looked impressed. "Good for you. Are you sticking around this summer?"

"Yes. My folks own Mountain Cycle, at the other end of the mall. I guess I'll work for them."

"How about if I make you a better offer?"

Sean put down his drink. "Excuse me?"

"A job. I'd like to hire you. I need someone to assist with repairs when my regular guys take vacations and to fill in on the sales floor."

Sean couldn't believe his ears. "You're offering me a job? Here?"

Mr. Payson laughed. "If your folks can spare you. I can use someone capable like you, who has some initiative. You could start next week. Are you interested?"

Interested! Sean was thrilled. He couldn't believe that someone wanted to pay him for doing what he loved to do for free. "Yes, Mr. Payson. Of course."

Suddenly they both noticed that Jay had crept up to the other side of the counter. He was trying to look like he was cleaning, but it was obvious that he was eavesdropping.

Mr. Payson turned around. "Jay, do you need something?"

"No." Jay pretended to wipe the same spot about ten times.

Mr. Payson took off his glasses and sighed. "Look, Jay, this is Sean Pendleton. He's going to start working for us next week." Payson glanced at Sean. "Sean, would you mind checking up on Jay's work every morning and reporting back to me?"

Sean loosened his grip on the old Levi's. "No, sir."

Jay's face was looking like an overripe tomato.

"Did you hear that, Jay?" Payson reminded. "Starting next week you talk to Sean every night. Ask him what needs to be done, and then he'll check it in the morning." When Jay just stood there gape-mouthed, Payson added, "Jay, do you read me?"

"I read you," Jay mumbled, starting to deflate.

Payson turned back to Sean. "Stop in whenever you can next week so I can introduce you to my repair men and show you around." He hopped off the stool and offered another handshake. "Welcome aboard."

"Thank you."

Mr. Payson went to attend to the last customer, and Sean and Jay stared at each other. Sean looked long and hard into those small eyes. But this time instead of seeing cockiness and strength, he saw only humiliation, jealousy, and fear.

Sean reminded himself of his mission, but somehow he couldn't do it now. He could only think about the years to come when he'd be at Cal Tech and Jay would still be here, emptying wastebaskets and having to answer to some kid who was even skinnier and younger than he was. Sean patted Jay's shoulder. "See you next week," he said with no sarcasm or malice. Before Jay could respond, Sean walked out.

It was still scorching hot as Sean trotted out of the mall and onto the downtown streets. Heading back to the van, he crossed the lawn in front of City Hall and ran into the sprinklers, letting the water drip down his face. Then he spotted an open Dumpster sitting by the curb, and he cruised over, lifting the old jeans high over his head and tossing them. Into the trash heap they flew, leaving barely a puff of dirt in their wake.

Sean strode on. That flagpole was beginning to seem like a tiny little island receding into some vast body of water. Jay was stuck on that island, but Sean realized now that he was sailing away.

CHAPTER 15

On Monday afternoon, Allie suddenly realized that she had made a mistake. A huge, terrible, dumb mistake. Thinking she could become an actress . . . maybe a french fryer at Burger King, or the toll-taker at the Golden Gate Bridge, but a professional actress? How could she become an actress when she was so nervous before her senior talent show that she could barely say her own name?

Brooke popped her head in the dressing room. "Ten minutes. We start in ten minutes," she announced in a cheery voice. Her overalls were dabbed with paint from some last-minute set touch-ups, and there was a hammer hanging from the loop on her hip. "Anybody need anything?" she called down the row of mirrors.

The other girls in the dressing room chirped, "No. We're fine."

Brooke checked her clipboard. "Al, I think we

fixed the dinosaur. Hopefully he won't knock you over or fall on you or anything. But I make no promises. You know how temperamental dinosaurs can be. Break a leg."

"Okay." Allie wiped bubbles of sweat from her forehead and stared into her mirror, which had a smile decal and a good luck message from the other girls written in lipstick. Penny, Terry, and Ursula were giggling and trading makeup, but Allie merely stared at her round face as if she'd never seen it before.

She knew that this performance was just for fun. And it was only her class out there, some of their parents, and a few teachers. No one who could affect her future or her career or her standing at the acting conservatory next year. Still, her stomach was churning like a washing machine and she could barely swallow. She was more nervous than she'd been for *Our Town*.

"Hey, Urs, what are you getting for graduation?" Penny was chattering.

"I asked for a car and a trip to Europe."

"Really?" the other two gasped.

"I'm getting a watch."

Terry and Penny laughed.

"Every time I mention the word graduation my mother starts crying," said Terry. "She got here early today to make sure she could sit in the front row, and what'll you bet she cries through the whole thing."

"She's losing her baby," teased Penny.

Now they were all singing and giggling and snapping the garters they wore in the junior sketch. Too nervous to join them, Allie dabbed on two last puffs of blush and slipped into the hall.

But it was just as crazy out there. Sean was yelling something about which wire went where in the PA system, and Brooke was carrying a stack of hats that was twice as tall as she was. Allie wove through the chorus kids, Sally Ann on her roller skates, and Bob Barnett with his juggling balls until she reached the door that led backstage. She pushed. At last — privacy. It was dark and musty like an old closet, and she could hear the buzz of the audience and the steady hum of the PA speakers. She felt her way over to the wall, behind the teaser curtains, and crouched.

She was suddenly so scared . . . terrified — of the future, change, the unknown, herself. She'd been so confident with her dad, assuring him that she had the stuff to make it as an actress. But how did she know that? Oh sure, she'd become the star of the drama department over the last year, but this was high school. What did high school have to do with real life? If she even managed to go to the acting conservatory, she'd probably find out the first day that every other student was much more qualified than she was.

And she'd been so sure that she could support herself, do it all on her own. So far she wasn't even close to finding a job and the more she thought about it, the more tightly she clutched her knees and the more lost and frightened she felt.

The velvet curtain rustled behind her, but Allie still didn't want to talk to anyone so she scooched forward to peek at the audience. She saw Meg handing out programs with Patrick. Meg's smile was forced and her movements stiff. Allie briefly wondered if Meg could be wrestling with senior panic, too. No, she decided. Meg was always so steady, so sure of herself. Allie spotted Sean's parents and Brooke's with two of her little sisters. And she saw Nick, sitting in the back surrounded by his admiring newspaper buddies, yet somehow looking as strained and unhappy as Meg.

Then Allie felt a gentle hand on her shoulder and she frowned, not wanting to interrupt her solitude. But when she saw who it was, some of her fear started to ease.

"Cici."

"Here you are," Celia whispered. "I've been looking all over for you."

"Hi." Allie's mind was flooded with memories of their times together when they were younger. The sculptures they'd created out of thrift store junk and summer flowers. The hours they'd spent in the old tree house with Sean, Meg, and Nick.

"I wanted to wish you luck. And to give you this." Celia held up the freshman fundraiser button that Brooke had worn to the frat party. "I thought you could wear it for the freshman part of the skit."

Allie took it from Celia and pinned it to her dress. "Thanks. I wouldn't have wanted to lose this." She patted the button. "It sure was a long time ago, wasn't it."

"What?"

"Freshman year."

"Oh, yes. A lifetime." Celia touched Allie's hand. They sat very still for almost a minute. "Al, your hands are freezing."

"I know. I'm so nervous."

"Why?"

"I keep thinking how this is the last time I'll sit at those mirrors. The last time I'll perform at Redwood High. I guess I feel like I'd better get it right."

"I know what you mean," Celia sighed. "There isn't much time left."

Then there was a crack of light as the side door flew open and the rest of the cast flooded into the wings. Feet scuttled, there was whispering and muffled giggles, and Allie could hear the hum of the speakers get louder and Brooke out in the hall, calling, "Places!"

"I'd better get out of here," Celia said, giving Allie a quick hug. "You'll be great."

" 'Bye."

Celia waved and squeezed her way out.

"Here we go," Allie mumbled to herself as she jostled to her place and waited for her first cue. Now her blood was speeding and her hands were numb. Her mouth was like dry sand and she wanted to bolt, only her feet wouldn't move. Then the lights dimmed over the auditorium and the crowd shushed each other until a few laughed and there were hoots and claps. The hum of the speakers got louder until there were cracks and pops and then the *2001* theme roared in her ears. Her cue. I'll never do it, Allie panicked. I won't go out there. I'll run away like I did junior year. Or I'll just stay in the wings and I'll never utter another word to anyone for the rest of my life.

But the next thing she knew, she was on the stage, in the middle of the warm, pink light. She felt the expectation, the delight of the people watching. Her fear was still there, but it didn't seem to matter anymore. It was just background noise like the music coming out of Sean's speakers. She cocked a goofy pose, the dinosaur jerked into place, and she began in a clear, confident voice, "Back in the days of the Stone Age, there was an early species of man called freshman."

The chorus kids hurried in behind her and laughter filled the auditorium — a round, joyful sound. Allie felt her fear turn to excitement until she realized she wasn't even afraid anymore. She hadn't made a mistake. Because no matter what her father or anybody else in the world thought — she was sure. It wouldn't matter if it was Redwood High or the acting conservatory or a stage somewhere far away. Here, in the light and warmth and laughter — this was where she belonged. This, for her, would always be home.

"You were great!" Brooke screamed in Allie's ear.

"Did it go okay?" Allie demanded.

"Okay?" Sean cried. "You and the dinosaur were brilliant!"

They were in the middle of onstage, post-talent-show madness. They were juggling balls on the floor and Sally Ann was still on her roller skates and Penny looked like she was doing a war dance. They'd done it! It was over. The Class of '88 Talent Show was an unqualified hit.

Sean was lifting Brooke up and swinging her. "I loved it when the dinosaur almost fell over, and you did that double take," he called to Allie. "I laughed so hard I almost fell over the speaker."

Allie started laughing and tears sprang down her cheeks. They were the same funny tears that had appeared during the last sketch, the part where she was a senior and had to say good-bye to everything at Redwood High. The tears kept coming, even though Allie felt anything but sad. She merely wiped the tears away and kept laughing and hugging and exchanging compliments with the other performers.

But in the midst of the hoopla and the hugs, she noticed a face down off the corner of the stage that did not compute. She stared and stared, knowing that it was a face as familiar as her own, but it was one she couldn't put together with the cardboard dinosaur and the juggling balls and Ursula and Terry whooping like cranes.

Her father.

"Dad, what are you doing here?" Allie said, breaking away from her friends and climbing down to meet him. He had his hands in his pockets and didn't quite look at her. Allie tensed. She was in some kind of trouble again. Her father was there to lecture her or drag her home.

"I came to watch your talent show," he said.

Instead, he shocked her.

Allie was speechless. Of course all the parents had been invited, and she'd dropped about a million hints to him and her mom about how she wanted them to come. But after they'd missed her in *Our Town*, the senior play, and the spring musical, she hardly expected him to show up now.

"Your mother arranged to get off at the bank," he explained. "But then she couldn't get a sitter for Emily. So it's just me."

Allie still stared at him, totally amazed that he was there. "That's okay."

' "I wasn't going to come. But I ran into Celia at the college yesterday, and she told me how determined you are. She said some things that convinced me to come."

"Celia convinced you?"

He nodded.

"Celia," she repeated to herself. "So," she managed shyly. "What did you think?"

"I think . . ." He paused. "I think I have a very talented daughter." She hopped down to hug him, but he held her back. "Don't jump to any conclusions, though. I have to talk this whole conservatory thing through with your mother. As far as I'm concerned, you're still going to Redwood College."

Allie didn't say a word.

He flinched as Ursula let out an ear-piercing shriek. Sean had put Talking Heads over the PA and kids were starting to dance. Mr. Simon backed away as if the sound hurt his ears. "I've got to get back to school now. But, well, I was very impressed. And proud."

"Thank you, Dad," Allie said. And then again after he left she whispered, "Thank you so much."

As soon as the lights came up after the talent show, Celia left the auditorium and began walking downtown. She was almost embarrassed at

174

how deeply that last sketch had hit her. She knew that everyone would be in high spirits as soon as the curtain went down, but she felt none of their joy or relief. She just kept thinking how there was so little time left. So little time.

It was still about a million degrees, but inside The Beauty Place, where her mother worked, the air conditioner was on overdrive. The women gossiped loudly enough to be heard over the fan, and as usual, her mom's voice was loudest of all. There were those silly pictures of out-of-date hairstyles on the walls and that stifling smell of nail polish and permanent wave solution.

"Do you have an appointment?" asked the woman at the desk.

"I'm here to see my mom. Jody."

"Oh. You're Jody's girl!" she bubbled. "You should come and visit us more often. I always forget that Jody has such a pretty daughter."

Celia gave a tight-lipped smile while the woman padded over to the line of swivel chairs and sinks. Celia's mom was pulling clumps of hair through holes in a rubber cap and smothering them with auburn goo. The woman underneath it all looked like she was going through shock therapy. Her mom excused herself when she saw Celia and came over.

"Hi," she said, surprised to see her daughter. She wore rubber gloves that were dripping with hair dye. "Is something wrong?"

"No." Celia looked at the floor. She wasn't quite sure what she was going to do now that she was here. She just knew that it connected to that old feeling—the one where she couldn't touch bottom. She knew that if she didn't make a final effort right now she might dog-paddle aimlessly in that scary, lonely place forever.

"Do you need the car, Cici? The keys are in my purse."

"I don't need the car."

Her mom blew her dyed bangs away from her eyes. "I have to get back to work. You don't exactly drop by to see me every day. What do you want?"

"It's about graduation," Celia said.

Her mom looked alarmed. "There's no problem, is there? Your grades are fine, aren't they?"

"Of course. There's no problem."

"Then, what is it?"

Celia gestured for her mother to move away from the front desk. They sat down together in the waiting area. Her mother held her gloved hands out in front of her and looked impatient.

"I wanted to let you know that the ceremony is at one on Friday. In the football stadium."

Her mother rolled her eyes. "Cici, don't worry. I won't be there. After you've begged me not to show up at your school since you were a freshman, do you really think I'm going to sneak into your graduation just to spite you?" She took a deep breath to cork her annoyance. "I'm working on Friday anyway."

"Could you get off?" Celia asked softly, her voice catching in her throat.

"Get off?"

"Could you maybe not work on Friday?"

Her mother looked right into her eyes. Behind

the heavy makeup Celia saw hurt, anger, and an awful lot of love. "Why?"

"I'd really like it if you did come to my graduation. I guess what I mean is, it would mean a lot to me if you could be there."

"It would?"

"It would."

"Well." Her mom cleared her throat and tried to pretend that she wasn't on the verge of tears. "I guess I could change my Friday appointments to another time. I guess I could do that."

"Thanks."

Mrs. Cavenaugh glanced back at her client in the rubber cap. "I'd better get back to Mrs. Shisgal or her hair won't just be streaked, it'll be fried." She turned back. "Are you sure you want me there?"

"I'm positive. Are you sure you can come?"

Her mom smiled shyly. "I wouldn't miss it for anything."

CHAPTER
16

Row after row of blue and white squares. Flowing blue robes on the boys and white robes on the girls with funny flat caps and red tassels hanging over their faces. All of them sitting in chair after gray metal chair like a grid across the football field. In front a small stage with Principal Peters and Miss Meyer, Joanne Fantozzi, Sean, and the other speakers. The boys steaming in shirts and ties under their robes and the girls trying to stay cool in new dresses and nylons under theirs. The freshly cut grass and florist flowers mixed with after-shave, heavy air, and a senior class worth of nervous sweat. And the music just ending. The long, brassy march finally over. Time for the ceremony to start.

Meg sat thirty rows back, between Alan Mc-Caffry and Gloria McGee. Alan kept jiggling his knee while Gloria snapped bubble gum. Meg couldn't blame them for not acting the way you were supposed to act at graduation, however that was. It was not only hot, but humid, and they were already worn out from the rehearsal that morning. They'd had to stand in line forever, making sure they stayed in perfect order. So each time Meg had seen Celia or Allie or Sean or Patrick — or Nick — she could only offer a limp wave and move on like a heifer in a herd. Of course, what would she do if she were able to stop and chat? Throw her arms around Celia, Allie, and Sean. But Patrick and Nick? She would just look at them both, wish them well, and shrink back into the sticky heat.

They all stood for the Pledge of Allegiance. The crowd in the bleachers stood, too, and Meg looked for a familiar face among the white dresses and summer suits. But the stands were packed, and she couldn't hope to pick out her parents. The longer she stared the more everything turned into one big blur.

Then the madrigal singers sang a hymn and the class song. Principal Peters welcomed everyone and talked about this being an end. And a beginning. One salutatorian spoke about freedom, another about responsibility. Finally, Sean's voice filled the stadium and Meg sat up.

He sounded confident, and from where she was sitting, she could make out his handsome profile. His cap sat proudly on his head, and he didn't fumble with his notes. He spoke firmly. Learn from your trials, your weaknesses. Find what's important and meaningful and hang on to it with

179

all your heart. Have the courage to embrace the future and to let the mistakes of the past go.

The guest speaker got up to talk about making a difference, but it started to jumble together in Meg's head. She kept hearing Sean's strong voice over and over, as if he'd been talking only to her. Or only to the five of them who'd started this journey together but were finishing it apart.

Roll call. Principal Peters mispronouncing names, just like everyone said he would. Meg's line was standing. No turning back now. It was like a river, one that she'd been swept up in a long time ago. Alan hesitated and Meg bumped into him. Then Gloria bumped into Meg and it was like a train that had just coupled on a track, the bump going through all the cars. Soon they chugged ahead and Meg was at the podium, her name being called. She heard her parents holler for her. She shook Principal Peters' hand. Then she followed the line as it snaked back. She listened to Sean's name and Nick's when they came to the R's. Joanne made a short farewell speech. And Meg moved her tassel from one side to the other like everyone else, and she even cheered and pitched her hat into the air.

It ended with Principal Peters giving his blessing, saying go out in the world and embrace change. Be brave. Meg's legs took her up to the stands where her parents hugged her and cried. But she stood limply. Not crying. Not laughing. Barely feeling alive. Because she knew she wasn't being brave or embracing change or letting her mistakes go. She didn't deserve to graduate. She was nothing but a sham.

＊　＊　＊

"We did it!" Celia yelled, throwing her cap in the air for what seemed like the fiftieth time. It came back down and landed with the corner planted firmly in the lawn. "Oops," she giggled, falling over Allie and Brooke. They were surrounded by parents and other seniors, all hugging and hollering and snapping picture after picture after picture.

"How was my speech?" Sean asked.

"THE BEST," all three girls said at the same time.

Greg Kendall and Sam Pond jumped Sean from behind, congratulating him and introducing him to their brothers and sisters, including a gurgling baby who was handed to Sean, who he had no idea what to do with.

Allie rushed off to meet her parents near the gate. Celia and Brooke stood together comparing diplomas until Celia looked up and saw her mother coming toward her. Her mom was in a pale sleeveless dress and heels and had that sentimental, teary expression that every mom seemed to be wearing. Except that every mom didn't also have a dyed punk hairdo and purple fingernails.

"You were great," Mrs. Cavenaugh said, giving Celia a tentative hug.

Celia reached up and hugged her back. "Mom, do you know Brooke Appleton? She's Sean's girl friend."

"I think I've seen you in front of Sean's house." Mrs. Cavenaugh smiled. "Congratulations."

"Thanks."

Sam and Greg stopped clowning to stare at

181

Celia's mother. Celia took a deep breath, then stuck out her arm and tugged them over. "Hey, you two madmen," she teased, "come meet my mom."

They both grinned and shook her mom's hand. Sam looped both his tassel and Greg's over his earlobes like dangly jewelry. "Pleased to meet you."

"Nice to meet you both," Mrs. Cavenaugh laughed. She looked up and waved. "There's Nick. NICK!! Over here!"

Nick was uncertainly making his way through the crowd, looking pale even under his sunburn. His tie was loosened and he'd already taken off his cap and gown. "Hi, Aunt Jody," he said, squeezing his way through to kiss her cheek.

"Congratulations, Nick." They looked at each other for a moment, then hugged.

"Have you seen Meg?" he asked Celia, wiping sweat from his face.

Celia batted Sam with her cap and giggled. "Not since we got our diplomas." She stood on her tiptoes to search. "I thought I saw her dad. But who could find anybody now?" She stuck out her tongue as Greg put his mother's camera in her face.

Nick moved away, pulling his aunt with him. "Aunt Jody, where's my mom?" He'd found his father and left him with Councilman Butler, the guest speaker. He'd guessed that his parents hadn't come together.

"Your mom and I drove together," his aunt confessed. "She was looking for you over by the stage."

He started to go.

"Hey, Nick," Celia called. "Let's meet at my house at around six and all go to grad night together."

Nick's face went ever paler. "Who's going?"

"You know. Me, Allie, Sean, and Brooke. Maybe Meg and Patrick."

Nick wilted. He was standing right in the flow of traffic, yet totally unaware that people were having to duck and dodge to get around him.

His aunt reached out to him. "Go to grad night, Nick," she urged softly. "Don't stay home and stew. It won't help. Go out and celebrate. Have a good time."

Nick looked at her hard, finding a wisdom in her eyes that he'd often seen there. Maybe it came from facing what was difficult in life. Nick had been thinking about that ever since Sean's speech. He used to assume that he was so much more mature than Sean — after all, he'd never been picked on or excluded. But listening to that speech he realized that he was the late bloomer and Sean was way ahead of him. Nick headed back into the crowd to look for his mother. Celia's voice stopped him.

"NICK, are you going to grad night with us?"

He took one last glance at his aunt and nodded. "I'll be over at six." Head down, he forced his way through the crowd.

Celia watched him until she saw Allie coming toward her, looking as bright and hopeful as Nick looked lifeless and confused.

Allie was carrying her four-year-old sister, Emily, who was wearing a ruffly pink dress and

Allie's graduation cap. "Celia! Cici!" Allie cried. "Guess what my dad said!"

"What?" Celia asked, sidling close enough to tickle Emily's leg.

"He's letting me go to the Conservatory. He and my mom talked it over. It's my graduation present. I have to work all summer, but he'll help me pay for it." She put Emily down and threw her arms around Celia, leaping and laughing. "You did it, Cici."

"Me?"

"He said it was seeing me act, that was what made him change his mind. And he wouldn't have gone if it weren't for you, if you hadn't told him to come."

Celia bit her lip and let her head fall back. She grinned at her mother, at Allie, at the crowded stadium, and the graying sky. "Gee, maybe I'm not such a fool, after all."

"And maybe I'm not such a nut case."

"Maybe," Celia laughed. And then they said at the same time, "But then again, MAYBE NOT!"

Nick went right home and waited in his living room. He sat forward on the old love seat and watched the ceiling fan. The air was so heavy now that the fan blades barely pushed through it and the lace curtains didn't flap. Almost no light came in through the windows, and it smelled like a thunderstorm.

Hughie barked when his father's Lincoln turned in, crackling along the gravel until it parked in the driveway. Nick sat quietly as his dad came in the back door. The refrigerator door opened, and there was the sound of liquid swishing in a pitcher and being poured into a glass. Soon his mother's Mercedes pulled in and the front door opened.

"Hi, Mom," Nick said. He could hear his father's footsteps come into the hall at the sound of his voice.

"I was looking for you in the stadium, but I thought I'd better go before this storm starts."

"I left early," he told her.

She put down her purse and came over to kiss him. "Congratulations." She sat next to him on the love seat. Her hair was in a neat page boy, and she wore a linen suit with expensive loafers. Her smile was as cool as ever, except for a slight trembling around the edges.

Nick's father entered the room from the opposite side. "I didn't know you were home already, Nick. Congratulations." He looked at Nick's mother and shifted uncomfortably. Staying in the doorway, he added, "I'm proud of you. We haven't talked about a graduation present. You should tell us what you want."

Nick couldn't resist the opening. "I want you to talk to me," he blurted. The words came out almost before he had planned to say them.

"About what?" his mother asked with not very convincing innocence. It was as if she were making one last effort at keeping up the smoke screen.

Nick took a deep breath and stared at his clasped hands. "I want to know what's going on. I've been hearing you fight like crazy for almost a year now, and everybody keeps acting like it's totally normal. Well, it's not normal. And I'm not

185

a kid anymore. I've graduated; I'm almost in college. I'm grown up. And I think I deserve to be told the truth." There was a long silence interrupted only by a far-off crack of thunder. Nick repeated, "Tell me what's going on."

His parents looked at one another. His mother's smile trembled away, and his father put his face in his hands. Then they both looked at Nick.

"All right," his father said very softly.

The ceiling fan pushed harder, making a slicing sound. Nick's mother twisted her wedding ring.

"I've said what I needed to say," Nick prompted, sitting up and looking at them. "Now I want you to talk."

His father began and Nick sat very still, knowing that the words would hurt, yet still winded each time he felt the stings and stabs. Then his mother spoke and Nick listened, barely breathing, hurting like crazy, and wondering how people recovered when things got this bad.

And when it was over he stood up and the blood rushed to his head. He'd heard everything he didn't want to hear. Everything he'd hoped to avoid. Yet he was still standing there. His parents were still his parents. He was still alive. He was just a little bit older.

Meg was a block from Patrick's when that first clap of thunder roared. She didn't alter her pace. Even when the water started to pour onto her graduation dress she strode steadily. Rain soaked her hair and dripped down her neck. Her shoes became spongy but she kept going, too filled with purpose to feel it or care.

She pounded Patrick's front door. She held the doorbell buzzer until she thought it would never stop buzzing. She leaned her head against his front door and cried, "Patrick, be home! Now! Please!" She was answered by another crack of thunder.

Patrick was probably out with his parents or still at school or already downtown helping figure out how to have grad night in this rain. Or maybe he knew why she was here and was purposely staying away, hoping she'd lose her nerve again.

But she wasn't losing her nerve this time. She'd stay here until tonight if she had to. Until the rain coated every inch of her body, until the gutters spilled over, until the water floated Patrick's house away. Meg slapped the door one more time with her wet hand, then looked out at the blurry street.

She saw it. Patrick's station wagon cutting a steamy trail through the sheet of water. It pulled up at the curb, the old brakes screeching, and the sudden silence as the radio was turned off. Meg didn't wait for him to get out. She ran across the wet grass, arriving at the passenger door as he was gathering his diploma and his suit jacket. She slid in next to him.

His long hair was wet, too, and the car smelled like damp blankets. When she pulled her door shut she watched the water stream down the windshield. Then she took his hand and made him look at her.

She saw it right away in his sweet, loving eyes. He knew what she was going to say. He'd probably known all along. Still, he didn't want her to say it. She cradled his hand in hers, and as the thunder cracked and the rain poured, she began to talk.

CHAPTER 17

The thunderstorm passed and the sky turned clear as cellophane. Downtown had never looked so clean, so new. The oldest blocks in Redwood Hills were roped off. Instead of shoppers and cars, there were celebrating seniors from five surrounding high schools, all dancing, eating, riding the rented carnival rides, and gearing up to party all night.

Nick stood in the street between the twangy guitar of The Spacemakers, a local band, and the screams coming from the Tilt-O-Whirl. He was with Celia and Allie and Sean and Brooke. The five of them stood in a huddle, warm and close.

"Nobody's getting tired, are they?" asked Sean, who had taken over Nick and Meg's old role as group leader.

Four voices pronounced a vigorous no.

"Good. So, who's daring enough to go on the dreaded hammer ride with me?" Sean pointed past the Ferris wheel to a ride that shot people up and down, then shook them up as if they were in a martini shaker. "This is where we separate the men from the boys." He smiled at Brooke. "Or the girls from the dinosaurs."

"I don't know," Celia paled, staring at the flashing lights and the giant hammer arm sweeping up and down.

Allie was already on her way. "Come on. We'll just scream a lot if it's too scary. That's the whole point of those things."

Celia still looked unsure, but Sean, Brooke, and Allie swept her along. Nick followed, too, not really caring about the hammer ride, but wanting to stay near his friends. But when they passed the Ferris wheel he stopped. His heart was suddenly in his throat and his limbs had started to come back to life.

"I'll stay here and watch," he told them.

"Oh, come on, Nick," Allie teased. "I've never known you to be a chicken."

"Somebody has to watch and then tell you how scared you looked, how you almost crashed and all that. That's how you're supposed to do it."

Allie let loose her crazy giggle. "That's the lamest excuse I've ever heard."

"Al," Sean prodded, "let's go. They're getting ready to start it again."

Brooke pretended to make Sean drag her. "Nick, if I don't come back, tell my sister Daphne she can have my toolbox."

They all stumbled into one another getting into line and waving at Nick, but Nick wasn't watching them. He was looking back, past the Ferris wheel, into the flickering light and the shadows. He was sure that he'd seen her, and he was also afraid he'd made a mistake. That's why he hadn't said anything to the others. He wasn't the only one who felt the big empty space of Meg's absence. They all missed her.

He watched the girl run closer, telling himself it could be the way the carnival lights shone down on the puddles, or just that he wanted to see her so badly. Then the outline of her body became more clear, and he heard her lightning swift footsteps. Meg.

Nick didn't move. He stood in the cool night air and waited for her to come to him. She finally stopped a few feet away. Strands of hair swept down her face. Her mouth quivered. She looked like she'd been crying, and yet her eyes were very clear.

"Where's Patrick?" Nick asked, barely breathing.

"He stayed home."

Nick's heart was pounding so hard he thought it would knock him over. "Why?"

"He didn't want to come. He's leaving in a few days for summer school at Cornell. He wanted to be with his family."

"You told him, then? About us?"

"Yes." She still stood an arm's length away. "He knew. He almost seemed relieved. He'd already been changing his mind about Cornell. I think he needed to be told about us so he could make the decision. It was hard, though."

"I know." He reached out his hand. She slowly extended hers, too. The tips of their fingers touched. "I talked to my folks."

"What did they say?"

"What I thought. What I hoped they wouldn't say. They're going to separate. I think they've been unhappy for a while. They both said they were waiting until I graduated to do anything."

"Until we graduated," Meg echoed, letting her head fall back. "Why have we all waited so long?"

"I don't know."

Then there was no more to say. Meg stepped in and rested her forehead on Nick's chest. She took a deep breath and smoothed her cheek along the soft cotton of his shirt, as if for the first time she had the luxury of taking him in slowly, with all her senses. Gently, he wrapped his arms around her and buried his face in her long hair. They stood like that, under the flickering light, until all sound, all color, all sense was gone. It was just them.

They kissed, not parting until they realized that four people were standing close and staring. The world came back into focus, and Meg's heart swelled to see Celia, Brooke, Sean, and Allie, backlit by a streetlamp and gawking. Sean and Brooke were grinning. Allie was stifling giggles. Celia looked shocked.

"Meg," Allie bubbled, breaking the silence. "I'm so glad you're here."

"It looks like you're not the only one," teased Sean.

Celia still looked at Meg and Nick as though she didn't quite understand.

Sean nudged her. "Are you surprised?" He looked at Meg and Nick. "I've known about you two forever."

Celia slowly grinned, her brain finally putting it together, then Allie giggled again. Brooke pulled her away, obviously embarrassed and wanting to give Meg and Nick a few more minutes alone. "That last ride was so great, we're sacrificing Allie to the Tilt-O-Whirl," Brooke said, gesturing to the others. "Come find us there in a few minutes. Okay?"

Nick and Meg nodded, staying behind. They stared at one another, both not quite sure this was finally happening.

"What are you going to do about your parents?" Meg wondered.

Nick touched her cheek. "There's nothing I can do, just deal with it. It is strange to have so many things ending."

"Maybe it's like they said today at graduation. Maybe it's not really an end."

"Not for us," Nick breathed, pulling her to him and kissing her hair, her cheek, her mouth. "For us its definitely the beginning."

By five that morning the trash cans were overflowing, and there was an occasional sandal or Redwood graduation program littering the downtown street. It was still dark and the gang trudged happily back to Sean's van. Only Brooke was really sleepy.

Sean gently helped her into the back. Allie and Celia sat up front, while Meg and Nick nestled together next to Brooke, who conked out as soon as the van started moving. Sean drove slowly, stopping at Brooke's house first. He carried Brooke in, not waking her, reappearing a few minutes later. "Where to next?"

"I guess my house and Nick's," Allie yawned.

Sean started the motor, which sounded incredibly loud on the empty street. The van sluggishly drove toward the bigger houses, the sprawling ranches, and open land. When they passed the Barricelli vineyard the first hint of a sunrise peeked up over Capitola Mountain. The paved roads turned to gravel, and there was the occasional cow moo or bird flutter. When they pulled into Nick's driveway, Hughie was already racing out to greet them.

Allie opened the door, allowing Hughie to jump in and scramble back to Nick and Meg. The pair bolted up to embrace him, and then they all sat quietly, listening to Hughie pant and the wind lightly rustle the trees.

"I don't feel like going home yet," Celia finally admitted.

"Me, either," agreed Allie.

Sean stretched back in the driver's seat with his arms behind his head. "We could go get some breakfast."

Nick nodded. "Or walk in the woods and watch the sun come up."

"I know!" Meg gasped. She was on her knees, holding Hughie and gazing out the window. She looked back at the others and bit her lip. "Anybody feel like visiting our old tree house?"

For a moment they all stared at her. The tree

house. Their childhood meeting place. They'd said good-bye to it four years ago when they entered Redwood High. Did it even still exist?

"Is our old tree house still standing?" Celia asked.

"Yes," Nick answered in a soft, sure voice.

Meg led the way out of the van. "Let's go."

They walked in a line, past the apple orchard and around the swimming pool and back to Hughie's doghouse. The oak trees were stocky and lush, their leaves almost hiding the tree house completely. But it was still there. The old planks they used as steps were still nailed to the tree trunk and the floor was just visible above the thick branches and heavy leaves. Nick helped Allie and Celia climb first.

Halfway up, Celia kicked off her high heels and they sailed down into a pile of leaves below. She pulled herself onto the floor, then extended a hand to Allie, who scooted up next to her.

"Hey," said Sean, climbing up next. "My old radio's still up here. I wonder if it still works."

"It does," Nick guaranteed.

There was silence. Meg looked at him. "How do you know?" she finally asked.

Nick shrugged and looked beyond the tree house, into the morning sky. "I know," he said.

He did know. The radio worked. It played pretty clearly considering that it was over thirty-five years old. The five of them huddled around it listening to the graduation dedications going out over KWRH to seniors from all the different high schools. Apparently they weren't the only ones still up and awake this morning in Redwood Hills.

The sky was pink and dusky. The leaves were blowing and the floor creaked. The space seemed smaller than anybody remembered it, and they huddled close like people stranded on a life raft.

"You know, I don't think all of us have been up here together since we were freshmen," Meg sighed, leaning back against Nick and snuggling.

"Yeah, the night Jay Creary got me," Sean said. "It looks a lot better to me now than it did then."

They all smiled. Actually, the tree house didn't look bad. Sure it was old and cramped — the wood had turned a dull gray and some of the nails were beginning to rust — but it was clean and well ordered.

"Somebody must have come up here and checked on this place," Celia said.

"I said I would," Nick admitted quietly. Meg cocked her head back to look at him. "Four years ago. I said I'd take care of the tree house. So I did."

They listened to more dedications. Then KWRH played "Graduation Girl," a corny song that had been a hit when they were sophomores.

"Remember this song?" Sean asked, shaking his head.

They all listened.

"Can you believe we made it? We really graduated," said Celia.

"I almost didn't," Allie giggled.

"We all had our moments," said Nick.

"And we're all still here," said Meg. "Together."

They quieted until the song was over, then shifted — Meg and Nick cuddling even closer, Celia and Allie leaning against each other's backs, and Sean crouching by the tree trunk, looking down at the top of the doghouse and the layers of leaves.

"My folks are splitting up," Nick suddenly told the others. Allie was the only one who looked surprised. "They want to sell the house."

They all sat up. "What about the tree house?" Sean asked.

Celia frowned. "Maybe we should finally take it down."

Allie nodded. "It is getting pretty old. The next big lightning storm might really do it in."

Sean looked each of his oldest, closest friends in the face. "Let's take a vote. I say, let it stand. Allie?"

She thought for a moment. "I guess the new owners should be the ones to decide."

"Celia?"

"Allie's right. Some new kids might want to use it."

"Nick?"

"I won't take it down."

"Meg?"

Meg rose to her knees and stretched her arm, placing her hand in the middle of the floor. Four other hands joined hers and they all knew they weren't talking about the tree house. It was something so much stronger and deeper. Something

197

that would take more than lightning or age to tear it apart. She looked at each of her friends, ending with Nick.

"It doesn't matter," Meg said quietly. "I think it will always be here, whether we take it down or not."

"I think so, too," Nick agreed. He looked at all of them. "In fact, I think it will be here forever."

Forthcoming teenage fiction
published in Armada

Class of 88 1–4
Linda A. Cooney

In A Spin
Mark Daniel

Nightmare Park
Linda Hoy

Sin Bin 1–4
Keith Miles

Run With the Hare
Linda Newbery

ARMADA

STEVIE DAY SUPERSLEUTH
(that's me!)

I'm on my way to being the first female Commissioner of the Metropolitan Police. It's true I have a few personal problems: for a start I'm small and skinny and people are always mistaking me for a boy. I'm 14 – though you wouldn't think so – and my younger sister, Carla, not only looks older than me but she's much prettier too. Not that that really matters. You see, she doesn't have my brains.

If you want to see my razor-sharp mind in action or have proof of my brilliant powers of deduction then read about my triumphant successes in:

STEVIE DAY: Supersleuth
STEVIE DAY: Lonely Hearts
STEVIE DAY: Rat Race

Have you seen
NANCY DREW
lately?

Nancy Drew has become a girl of the 80s! There is hardly a girl from seven to seventeen who doesn't know her name.

Now you can continue to enjoy Nancy Drew in a new series, written for older readers – THE NANCY DREW FILES. Each book has more romance, fashion, mystery and adventure.

In THE NANCY DREW FILES, Nancy pursues one thrilling adventure after another. With her boundless energy and intelligence, Nancy finds herself enrolling at a crime-ridden high school, attending rock concerts and locating the missing star, skiing in Vermont with friends Bess and George and faithful boyfriend Ned, and temping at a teenage magazine based in wildly exciting New York.

COMING IN SPRING 1988

The Nancy Drew Files

No. 1 Secrets Can Kill
No. 2 Deadly Intent
No. 3 Murder on Ice
No. 4 Smile and Say Murder

ARMADA

On the Spot
Mark Daniel

Ben O'Connell has a problem. He is small. Humiliated at home and bullied at school, he seems a born loser. But Ben has a special talent for snooker and he's determined to reach the top.

It seems that no one can beat him and nothing will stand in his way – until scheming Perry Curling becomes his manager. To him, a boy like Ben is made for hustling round seedy snooker joints. Winning championships, says Curling, is the stuff dreams are made of. After all, this is tough '80s Merseyside.

But Ben is aiming for the top . . .

An Armada Original